OLD WORLD SAGA

FEAR THE FULL MOON

AN OLD WORLD SAGA NOVELLA

FEAR THE FULL MOON

Copyright © 2023 by Joel Preston.

First edition published 29 December 2023.

Book cover art by warrendesign
Manuscript design by Joel Preston

ISBN 978-0-6457791-3-4 (Paperback)
ISBN 978-0-6457791-4-1 (eBook)

To contact the author email: contact@joelprestonauthor.com
joelprestonauthor.com

OLD WORLD SAGA

FEAR THE FULL MOON

AN OLD WORLD SAGA NOVELLA

JOEL PRESTON

This novella is dedicated to Pani and Ando. A cat for home and a dog for work leaves life in perfect balance.

OLD WORLD SAGA

IN READING ORDER

This novella takes place **between** The Old World Saga Book Two:
Rise Golden Apollo and The Old World Saga Book Three: **In the
Shadow of The Old World.**

For maximum enjoyment of this novella it is best to have read the preceding books
before beginning.

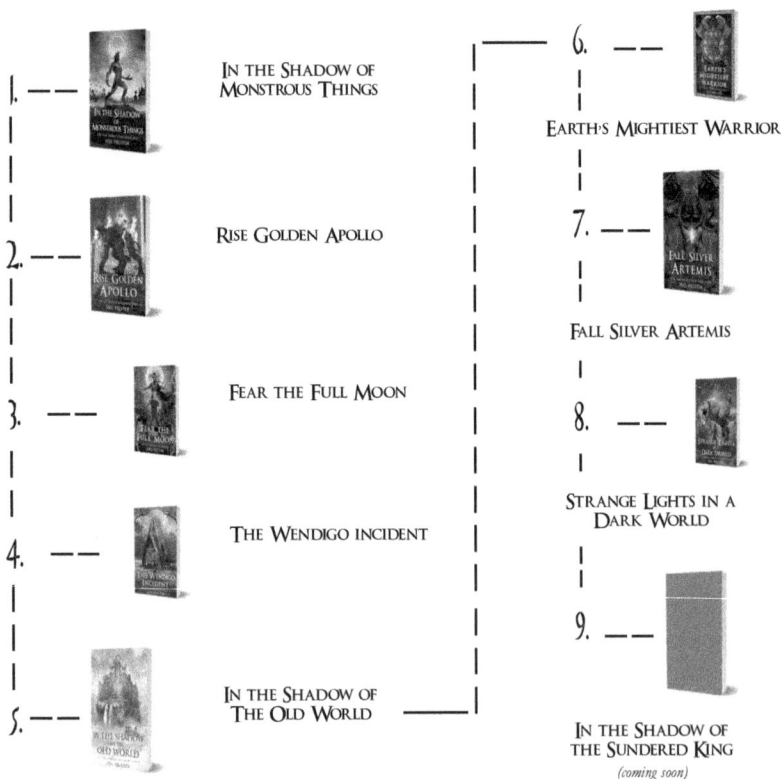

1. — IN THE SHADOW OF
MONSTROUS THINGS

2. — RISE GOLDEN APOLLO

3. — FEAR THE FULL MOON

4. — THE WENDIGO INCIDENT

5. — IN THE SHADOW OF
THE OLD WORLD

6. — EARTH'S MIGHTIEST WARRIOR

7. — FALL SILVER ARTEMIS

8. — STRANGE LIGHTS IN A
DARK WORLD

9. — IN THE SHADOW OF
THE SUNDERED KING
(coming soon)

PROLOGUE

- 2020 -
SOUTHEAST ASIA

Creeping along the oil-stained walls it knew so well, the large fat rat paused. Something was different. There was an unfamiliar odour in the air, though the vermin couldn't determine its nature.

The long shadows of the room carried an unusual sinister quality that made the rat's hairs prick up. Something was most certainly out of place. Still, the creature's rumbling stomach was too fierce to ignore. Little more than a slave to the whims of its hunger, the rat pressed on.

Hugging the wall tightly, it continued along its familiar path. The crumbling concrete pillars of the derelict building loomed over it as old friends in the gloom. Everywhere, the greenery of the jungle poked through the cracks. The tangled vegetation winding around rotten crates provided the perfect home for the colony of rats that dwelled here.

When the sounds of battle were silenced, the vermin's ancestors had moved in. War ended, and this place was abandoned by the humans who'd dwelled here. In the quietness of the concrete, the rats thrived, multiplying in their hundreds. They were safe from the abundant predators of the forest behind the solid walls.

The unfamiliar scent grew in intensity, so the rat stopped. Its hesitation proved lethal as it fell victim to a strike of unfathomable speed. It squeaked in panic as long thin fingers wrapped around its struggling torso and pulled it into the air.

The rat contorted its body, desperately trying to bite its unseen attacker, but it couldn't reach. Before it properly comprehended its peril, teeth bore down on its neck.

The attacker ripped the rat's head off and spat it away. It gnawed on the rat's body, consuming fur, flesh and bone with famished, gulping bites.

This unseemly creature in the dark was a man. His hair was long and matted with filth. His face was gaunt and his eyes hollow, carrying visions of untold horrors. Blood dripped down the scraggly strands of his beard onto his filth-laden poncho.

This was no man of the civilised world. At least he was no longer. He was wild.

Sometimes, he would hunt in the forest for prey. It was a difficult thing for a man to wrangle a deer with his bare hands, and then fight off the big cats that came to scavenge. The rats were easier. The rats were what he deserved.

There was a distant clap of thunder, and the man looked up into the black void of the ceiling. The rain was dangerous. Monsoonal flash floods threatened old structures like this. He was too close to the river. He had to move.

The man took another bite of the rat carcass and tossed it aside. He kicked up small plumes of dust as he made his way to the large metal doors of the bunker. Their rusty hinges squealed and protested as he pushed them open.

The outside filled him with a familiar mix of unease and despair as he perceived the gloom of the forest. The wild man turned his gaze to the sky and saw the moon shining high above.

It was almost full.

The time of change, of grotesque transformation beyond the knowledge of all science, was almost upon him again. He had to get away from even the barest semblance of civilisation. Back into the dark, malevolent depths of the jungle he would go.

The forest was home to many beasts, though none compared to him. He was the worst of the monsters of this land.

Vegetation had almost completely consumed the barbed wire fence surrounding the concrete bunker. The man ducked through the large hole that had granted him access, but paused when his foot hit something half-submerged in mud.

It was a sign or plaque that had fallen from its original perch. The man bent over and wiped the mud from its face. He couldn't read it, as the writing was faded beyond all recognition. What he could see, highlighted by the moon above, was his reflection in the dull glass.

He'd never seen himself like this.

"Who am I?" he thought.

A flood of memories came back to him. The man's mind raced back to the night it had happened. The night he'd faced a horror and lived to tell the tale.

The night he'd become a monster.

CHAPTER ONE

FLEE

Panic was the singular, overwhelming emotion flooding Jesse Billiau's mind. He glanced into the rear-view mirror and saw the squat tan Greek man in the back seat smiling at him. It wasn't a genuine smile, as the Greek's upturned lips carried relief, greed and concern. The man was sweaty; his stink climbing Jesse's nostrils and flooding his brain. He was revolting in more ways than smell. Still, an impossible series of events had forced the pair together.

Jesse breathed in deep as he turned hard right. His stolen vehicle skidded around the corner, briefly mounting the curb before straightening out on the highway.

"Do not drive so recklessly. We will get caught before we have a chance to flee," the Greek tutted as if Jesse was an impudent child.

"Flee," Jesse thought pensively. Flee to where, exactly? In the last thirty minutes, he'd been bitten, impaled by a supernatural monster, shot the thing dead, knocked out a government agent, and was now on the run. These were not normal circumstances, and as such, he had no idea where to flee to.

"What is your plan?" the Greek asked.

"I'll go home... see my girlfriend," Jesse mumbled, unsure.

"There is no time. We should go to the airport."

"No," he stated absolutely. His clothes were soaked with blood and they were in a stolen government car. They could be tracked easily and were too recognisable to just wander into the airport. Plus, the Greek in the back was in handcuffs.

"I've got a spare key at home. We will change cars, and I will unlock your cuffs," Jesse decided. This was good; a plan was forming in his mind.

"You are a smart man, knowing I am the only one who can help you now," the Greek grinned. There was that greedy and sinister smile again. Jesse's time as a cop had taught him not to trust people who smiled like that. As such, he didn't respond. It was true that the reason he'd wanted this car was due to the Greek's imprisonment in the back seat. He was potentially the only person in Cairns who, at least at this moment, didn't have the means to lock him up and turn him into a science experiment.

The irony of this situation didn't escape him, as it was only days ago that the Greek and his deranged accomplice, a man covered in scars, had kidnapped him. They'd lured Jesse to a seedy restaurant for an ambush, then taken him prisoner. He'd been tied up in an underground room and beaten.

Why?

To prompt his rescue by a friend, Joshua Dare. His kidnappers knew, much as Jesse did, that Josh wasn't an ordinary 23-year-old university graduate. The surreal truth was that Josh carried a curse that caused him to transform into a supernatural monster on the full moon. The Greek had been hunting Josh, as had the Australian Government. Jesse, through what seemed like little more than misfortune, had become wrapped up in the whole mess.

However, that wasn't strictly true. He'd let his paranoia build and put himself in harm's way. It was his fault his life was falling apart around him, at least in part.

Josh had rescued Jesse. And in the ensuing chaos, a different supernatural monster had come for them. Jesse had killed the monster, but not before it had bitten him, passing on its deadly curse. The curse was something from children's fiction, yet monsters in the moonlight had become his reality.

This time next month, Jesse would become the creature he'd killed. A werewolf... a creature from myth, made flesh. A horror that now lurked somewhere deep inside him.

"To the airport!" the Greek demanded, shaking him from his train of thought.

"Why the airport?" Jesse asked, barely hiding the contempt in his voice.

"The government men, or the police, will have you by the end of the night if we don't get out of the country."

"You have tickets?" Jesse asked.

"Yes," the Greek nodded. "For the Wolf of the Vatican and I."

"To where?"

"To the Vatican, eventually. We are going the long way round to avoid detection."

"Where is the first stop?"

"Vietnam."

"Will I be able to use the Wolf of the Vatican's ticket?"

"Yes. These are not ordinary tickets booked by an ordinary traveller, after all."

"Alright," Jesse capitulated. He couldn't come up with any better options without time to consider the full circumstances, and time was a luxury in short supply. He checked the mirrors to ensure they weren't being followed by any sleek black cars or police cruisers. In doing so, he glimpsed the full moon shining high above. That damned glowing orb had caused all of the chaos tonight.

With one hand gripping the steering wheel, Jesse ran the other along the myriad of fresh scars crisscrossing his body. His skin was marred where the monster had bitten him.

The Australian Government wanted to chain him up and use him as a test subject. The mysterious representative of the Australian Supernatural Taskforce, Liam Sager, had told him as much. They'd already captured his friend, Joshua Dare, who'd gotten Jesse into this mess. He was not going to suffer the same fate.

"Over my dead body," Jesse self-affirmed as he slammed his foot to the accelerator.

It only took minutes to reach his home.

With a wild swerve, the car skidded to a halt beside his driveway.

"Don't move," Jesse ordered the Greek.

Electronics," Jesse thought. He had to ditch his electronics. He didn't have a phone, as it'd been stolen when he was kidnapped, so he hastily took off his smartwatch and threw it into the garden.

Feeling foolish and unsure, Jesse made for the entry.

As he stepped through the front door, he was confronted by his girlfriend. Her face fell when she saw the blood coating him. Her eyes followed the significant scars on his exposed shoulder and arm.

"Kayla, listen," Jesse began, grabbing his partner on her shoulders. "I don't have much time. Do you know where my spare handcuff key is?"

She nodded, tears welling in her eyes.

"Go and get it, along with your car keys. I need my passport, too."

"But, why -"

Jesse tried to silence her with a stern look, the act proving to be a mistake.

"Don't you dare!" Kayla breathed, her aggravation apparent in her tone.

Jesse asked again, with a strongly emphasised 'please'. The obvious concern (though somewhat hidden by the mounting anger) in Kayla's eyes was justified, as Jesse had been a viral sensation over the last few days, and not for positive reasons. His kidnappers, the Greek and the Scarred Man, had posted a video of themselves attacking the bound and tortured Jesse to the internet. If he was in her shoes, he wouldn't go anywhere until he had answers.

"I'll explain, I promise," Jesse struggled to hide his exasperation.

Looking very confused and somewhat hurt, Kayla jogged off

to find the items he'd requested.

Jesse, meanwhile, sprinted to the shower. He had to clean himself up and change his clothes. There was no time to collect personal belongings as he knew the police would be here any moment. It was a miracle that he'd beaten them to this place.

It only took a minute to wash away the blood and get dressed. He pulled a long-sleeve t-shirt over his head and put on baggy jeans.

Kayla burst into the bathroom with Jesse's passport, handcuff key and her car keys.

"You got kidnapped!' she howled, releasing her inner distress in a tidal wave of emotion. "I've been so worried! What the hell happened? And now you just show up, all injured, without even saying hello!"

Jesse gripped Kayla in a tight embrace.

"I'll explain it all to you when I can," he attempted to reassure her.

"Explain now!" she demanded, pushing him away.

"I can't tell you, it'll put you in danger," Jesse urged, reaching for the car keys.

"It's to do with your friend, Josh, right? You've been obsessed with him for a month! Why? I know it was because of him you got kidnapped."

"Okay. Remember how I told you about the night in Pokers Hill? About what really killed Steve?"

Steve had been Jesse's mentor and had saved his life at the cost of his own.

Kayla nodded, wiping away a tear.

"It was a monster like I said. Now the government is coming for me. And if you know too much, they will come for you too. The kidnapping, everything, was all about the monster. This is way bigger than I can tell you."

Kayla did not look remotely convinced, but Jesse didn't have time. He heard the wailing of a distant police siren.

"I'll be back," Jesse whispered, kissing her on the cheek. "Do me a favour. When they get here, tell them that I have gone south. You have to be convincing, okay?"

Her expression was utterly unreadable, but there was no time for further instruction.

He darted out the front door, briefly looking back at the shaken and annoyed Kayla.

Jesse opened the rear door of his stolen car and pulled the Greek out, quickly undoing the cuffs.

The Greek massaged his wrists, which had turned slightly purple, then thanked Jesse.

"Don't thank me now," he murmured. "We aren't out of this yet."

"What now?" the Greek asked.

"We take my girlfriend's car to the airport. How long till the flight?"

"It is flexible. We had planned to leave tomorrow, though there is a flight tonight. We expected to have been done with the werewolf well before now, so that was another option."

"Good."

Jesse led the Greek to Kayla's small pink sedan. Against the rising backdrop of blaring sirens, Jesse left his home behind. As the old two-story house vanished from view, Jesse couldn't help but think that he was leaving life as he knew it behind.

He looked at the ominous full moon floating high above and cursed. He would face what was coming on his terms. Whatever horrors the next month would bring could be met once he was free.

CHAPTER TWO — FLIGHT

By some miracle, Jesse and the Greek made it to the airport unimpeded. The Greek produced his bizarre tickets, stamped with the seal of the Vatican city-state, which skyrocketed Jesse's anxiety. One call to the Federal Police and it was over for them. Fortunately, the Greek hadn't been searched by the AST, meaning his jacket pockets were still chock-full of his belongings. One item was Jesse's police ID, stolen from him during the initial kidnapping. Through negotiation skills he didn't know he possessed, Jesse was able to leverage his role as a police officer to get them on the shortly departing flight.

As the check-in person assessed their tickets (with more than just a degree of scepticism), Jesse couldn't help but notice that an odd man seemed to be keenly observing the pair from the far wall. He was tall, dark-skinned and even from a distance, somewhat imposing. Jesse considered that he was a government operative stationed at the airport in case something went wrong tonight. But that didn't seem right. The stranger had a funny aura that seemed to chill Jesse. His face was cast with shadow, yet his eyes were undoubtedly fixed on the pair.

Jesse brushed off his concern as paranoia from the night's events. The man wasn't coming over or trying to interact with them in any way. Yet, he continued to stare...

Of more pressing concern were the airline staff. Jesse's cop sense told him that the check-in guy would report their suspicious arrival, but hopefully not right away. It wouldn't take long for the government to put two and two together and deduce where the pair had gone.

In a blur of time and corridors, they were checked in, through security and onto the waiting plane.

Jesse sat back in his way-too-small seat, his heart beating in his ears. It couldn't be this easy, could it?

Jesse was a big guy. Standing at six foot eight and weighing 110 kilograms, he was a wall of muscle. It made airline travel uncomfortable at the best of times, without the added anxiety. He was tense, with dark pools of sweat dampening his shirt. He tried to breathe in deep and relax, but it was impossible. Every minute that passed before the plane took off intensified Jesse's panic. He was sure red and blue flashing lights were going to appear on the tarmac any second.

Then, Jesse's stomach dropped as he saw a police vehicle zoom by, escorting a string of black government cars.

It was over. He was done.

The convoy didn't stop. They passed Jesse's aircraft, heading towards a large military cargo plane parked across the main runway. A large truck rumbled along shortly afterwards. The gaps in its rear cargo hold, where slivers of light could escape, shimmered with a silvery glow, like it contained an enormous gleaming disco ball.

Jesse didn't need to guess hard to assume the truck's actual contents. His friend, Joshua Dare, currently lost inside the body of a monstrous black werewolf, was almost certainly in there. That hulking beast with its malevolent orange eyes was the government's main priority, not Jesse.

Jesse breathed a sigh of relief as the plane sped into the skies away from Cairns. Their destination, Hanoi, was the capital of Vietnam. By sheer impossibly good fortune, they'd escaped the city cleanly.

"Well done," the Greek yawned begrudgingly from the seat beside Jesse's. "I thought there was very little chance we would be successful. We have several other flights to the Vatican after we land in Hanoi."

"We aren't staying at the airport," Jesse hissed at the Greek, ensuring no one around them was listening in.

The Greek frowned. "It is important that we get to the Vatican as soon as possible."

"The government will be able to work out where we have gone very quickly. The Vietnamese authorities may be waiting for us on the other side of this flight. We get out of the airport, into the city."

"I don't like it," the Greek mumbled as he picked at his moustache.

"I don't care," Jesse growled.

"You need me now. No one else can help you. In one month, you will become death made flesh. You will listen to me."

"You will tell me what I need to know, then make your way

wherever you want to go by yourself," Jesse stated absolutely. Once he was well educated on his new affliction, he'd happily leave the Greek to be recaptured by the Australian Supernatural Taskforce.

The Greek began to argue but stopped when he noticed the person in front of them turn and gaze at the pair curiously.

Jesse glared at the Greek. They both understood they'd have to put a pin in this conversation for now.

It was going to be a long silent flight for Jesse Billiau as he pondered this unexpected turn of events. Was his path now headed for the Vatican? Was he any better off there? He simply didn't have enough information to make an informed decision.

"Whatever ensures my freedom," Jesse told himself.

Then, Jesse was no longer aboard the aircraft. He looked at his fingers, though they weren't familiar. Gone were his large, calloused and brutish hands, replaced with those of a child's.

"Hello," Jesse squeaked, the voice appearing as a memory brought to life.

It was dark and wet. Jesse was soaked up to his waist in swiftly moving water and could feel the chilly breeze whistling down the long concrete tube. While he couldn't see, Jesse could feel the iron bars pressed into his back. He was trapped in the unfathomable, cloying dark of the tunnel. His brothers had been playing in the rain, floating leaves as poor man's ships along the gutter and watching them descend into the storm drain.

Out of nowhere, water had ripped Jesse from his perch and sent him careening into the blackness. He'd surfaced, half-drowned in the abyss, forced against the iron bars by the strength of the current. Jesse was alone, hidden from the eyes of those who loved him by earth, cement and water.

Something splashed in the tunnel, and Jesse cried. He was utterly trapped, unable to defend himself from the things that lurked in the deep, even if he wanted to... The small boy was powerless against the rising torrent...

• • • • •

WITH A SQUEAK AND A CLUNK, the plane touched down at Noi Bai International Airport. The shaking of the aircraft woke Jesse from his sleep. He was secretly glad to be free of the unpleasant memories manifesting as dreams. An adrenaline dump had caused him to almost pass out once they'd reached cruising altitude. He looked at the Greek, who appeared alert. It almost seemed like the Greek had been watching Jesse, as he quickly turned his head to avoid meeting his eyes.

"What is your plan?" the Greek asked quietly, apparently eager to broach the topic of their escape again.

"I don't know," Jesse replied through gritted teeth. His mouth was dry and he had a slight headache, making him feel irritable. Did the Greek assume that he'd formulated a plan in his sleep?

"Luck will only take us so far," the Greek shrugged, a fact that Jesse was already well aware of.

Jesse looked across the aisle out the window and noticed through the grime that the tarmac was abuzz with activity. Small tugs trafficked large containers back and forth while people in hi-vis jackets attended to various tasks. It was abnormally crowded on both sides of the plane. And it was loud. Vehicle sirens were blaring as loudspeakers issued safety warnings. Jesse could use this; he just had to figure out how.

One of the flight attendants, a small woman with a pointed face, noticed Jesse's interest and informed him that Noi Bai Airport was going through significant airside upgrades and that the passengers would have to be careful when exiting the aircraft because of the high vehicle traffic.

"There is enough noise down there to get lost in," Jesse thought as he hatched a plan.

A couple of rows up, a particularly obnoxious couple were loudly debating the merits of social media pictures on their phones. It was clear they were influencers of some sort discussing how to best present Vietnam to their followers.

Jesse turned to the Greek and rather loudly exclaimed, "I am going to start documenting this trip from the moment we get off the plane. I reckon you've gotta begin the story with the plane on the tarmac."

The Greek looked perplexed, but Jesse was pleased to see the girlfriend murmur her agreement to her boyfriend about his remark.

Everything went like clockwork. Jesse made sure to stick close behind the pair, who promptly paused to take selfies on the walkway beside the plane. When they were swooped on by airline attendants in high-vis jackets, demanding they put their phones away, Jesse made his move.

He grabbed the Greek by the shirt and pulled him behind a parked tug. The pair then ran the length of its long train of containers, moving steadily away from the aircraft.

Another tug pulled in close, the driver noticing Jesse and the Greek, giving them a quizzical look.

The driver would've shouted if Jesse hadn't sprinted up and punched him in the side of the head. It wasn't a measured response, but it was the best idea he had. The Greek hopped in the passenger seat of the tug while Jesse, feeling quite guilty, left the unconscious man splayed out on the ground.

Before anyone was the wiser, Jesse was cruising along the airport's perimeter road towards the distant fence, feeling the wind in his hair. It felt like freedom.

Any second the alarm would be raised, but they'd be gone before then.

Jesse slammed the tug into the thin outer fence, damaging it enough that the two men could slip through the severed wires.

Again, by some miracle, they'd gotten out. They slithered into a vast network of industrial buildings before stumbling across a road. Jesse managed to wave down a passing taxi, who gladly accepted the Greek's cash.

"Where to?" the taxi driver asked, greedily eyeing the wad of money in the Greek's outstretched hand.

"Ahhh," Jesse stumbled over his words. He had no idea about Hanoi.

Fortunately, the Greek interjected on his behalf, "Take us to a hotel near Ta Hien Street. Any will do."

"Why there?" Jesse asked.

"Famous nightclub and party area near the Old Quarter. Easy to get lost in."

Jesse nodded his approval, and they were moving.

A few blocks back from the loud noise and boisterous crowds of Ta Hien Street was a small, somewhat run-down motel willing to take cash for a quick room.

The Greek and Jesse shambled up the stairs and pushed the stained yellow door open to find two mouldy beds against a water-damaged wall. The room reeked of stale cigarettes and looked like it'd been hastily vacated, as rubbish was strewn across the floor. It wasn't glamorous, but it'd do.

The Greek clearly wasn't impressed as he turned his nose up at the place.

However, once the door was shut, he forgot his disgust and rounded on Jesse, "We have delayed discussing this properly long enough."

Jesse frowned, half wanting to punch the small man as he had the tug driver. The Greek was far more deserving than the airport worker had been.

Jesse peered down at the short, fat, sweaty man without the merest pretence of trying to hide his contempt. The Greek had deep stains under his armpits and reeked of body odour.

The Greek on the other hand looked at Jesse with unmistakable greed. Jesse was a prize for him to claim and one he desperately wanted.

"We got out of Australia. That is all I wanted to do. You can go wherever you want now," Jesse snapped back.

"I cannot do that. I cannot return to the Vatican having both failed my task and without Dragan. What happened to him?" he demanded.

Jesse frowned. He didn't know who exactly Dragan was but could guess easily enough.

"The skinny werewolf? He's dead. I killed him," Jesse retorted, surprised at the maliciousness in his voice.

"But he got you. I saw the scars. You are his natural replacement," the Greek was positively salivating at this conclusion.

"I am not a stooge of the Vatican! I haven't just escaped becoming the AST's prisoner to be a prisoner of a different kind!"

Jesse suddenly realised he was shouting. He swiftly moved to the small open window on the far side of the room to close it. He was forgetting himself. He wasn't safe here and had to maintain a low profile. When he glanced onto the street below, he cursed his carelessness.

A man in a black suit with an obvious earpiece moved with haste along the footpath. It didn't appear as if the person had heard Jesse, as he was chattering quietly to himself. A large white vehicle, looking to be a luxury four-wheel-drive, was swiftly approaching the agent. The car stopped, and a very familiar person stepped out.

With his thin frame, tanned skin and surfer good looks, Federal Agent Liam Sager couldn't be mistaken for anyone else. To see him here, now, set alarm bells ringing.

Jesse swore. They'd been right on his tail the whole time. Jesse and the Greek must've only been one step ahead of them.

"Goddammit," Jesse murmured, pulling the curtain across the window.

The Greek pressed his thin lips together into a frown.

"Problem?"

"The AST are here. They followed us."

"They are good agents. They work quick."

Jesse had to privately admit that the Greek was right, but was reluctant to dump more praise than was necessary on their pursuers.

"I doubt they will search every hotel; they won't have the manpower. If we pay off the woman in the lobby, she will lie for us," the Greek yawned.

Jesse considered this suggestion and then dismissed it. "We can't trust that. We have to leave."

"You run from these men as if you are a sheep from a wolf," the Greek peered intensely at Jesse. "Why?"

Jesse didn't particularly want to dive into the depths of his psyche with the Greek. He had reasons for wanting to live free from iron bars in the dark, whether mental or physical. His experience in the water-logged tunnel as a child had made him eternally afraid of confinement. He smiled at the irony that he'd accepted a job as a police officer, a role in which he put people in literal cages. That was different, though. Those people deserved it.

"That isn't important right now. I think it's clear that we have to get out of Hanoi. Have you got money?" Jesse swiftly changed the topic.

"I have some US currency remaining, though not enough for a prolonged chase across Vietnam," the Greek sighed as if Jesse was being ridiculous.

Jesse ran his hands through his hair, feeling beads of sweat stick to his skin. They needed a vehicle. That much was clear. As they'd driven towards Ta Hien Street, the roads had been a sea of mopeds. They had darted through the narrow streets and around the abundant foot traffic.

Loud voices in Vietnamese burst out from a room nearby, carrying through the wall as if it wasn't there. The Greek moved to bang on the flimsy foundation, but Jesse stopped him. Again, Jesse saw the potential for an opportunity that could be exploited.

"Give me money," Jesse demanded.

The Greek eyed him warily but did as requested.

Jesse turned the slimy knob of their room and moved into the hall. He followed the loud, abrasive shouting until he arrived at another similarly seedy room entry.

Jesse banged on the door three times, then waited.

A small man emerged, dressed in nothing but his skin, looking utterly perturbed. His eyes were glassy and red from obvious intoxication. Jesse saw a scantily-clad woman dart away in the background. Perhaps a prostitute, though it didn't matter.

When the man looked up at the giant that was Jesse Billiau, confusion and fear crossed his face briefly before the same indignant rage re-emerged.

He began to shout, but Jesse silenced him by showing him the American bills.

"English?" Jesse asked.

The man nodded unsteadily, holding onto the door to maintain his balance.

"Downstairs, on the other side of this building, by a white car are white men in suits. I will give you this money if you distract them. Do you understand?"

The man nodded again, suddenly looking amused. He opened his palm, and Jesse thrust the crumpled notes into it.

True to his gestures, the little Vietnamese man bounded down the stairs with surprising gusto, apparently unaware that he was stark naked.

Jesse ushered the Greek to follow.

They waited in the foyer. For what Jesse wasn't sure, but he'd know when it happened.

Then, a series of annoyed shouts came from down the street. Australian accents were ordering someone to stop moving. A sound, suspiciously like shattering glass, reached Jesse's ears.

This was the sign to move.

"Lead us towards Ta Hien," Jesse whispered to the Greek.

The Greek hitched his pants up, checked the coast was clear, then strode into the Vietnamese night. Resigned to this improvised plan, Jesse followed.

They moved quickly and soon found themselves buried in an ocean of late-night revellers. Jesse stood out like a sore thumb, being so tall. He practically shoved people aside as the Greek led them into the beating heart of the nightclub district.

The bright lights and loud music were disorienting. Several women suggestively winked at Jesse as they passed, making him feel even more obvious. If a government agent saw them now, they were done.

A moped beeped, causing Jesse and the Greek to jump in fright. Two men, on scooters of green and yellow respectively, were trying to weave around them.

"Give us a ride?" Jesse asked the lead driver, practically shouting over the noise of the street. He'd been toying with the idea of potentially stealing mopeds, but this was even easier.

One of the men turned to the other with a look of casual disinterest, then shrugged. It was as if such a request was a common occurrence around here.

"Where to?" he asked Jesse cautiously.

"Out of the city," Jesse answered. Now wasn't the time to play games.

The scooter driver shook his head. Then, the Greek produced a hefty stack of American bills, and the man's attitude changed.

"Hop on," he grinned, shuffling forward to make space for Jesse.

The Greek didn't look pleased about this turn of events but hopped on the back of the other scooter regardless. Neither man fit well, Jesse due to his size and the Greek due to his protruding stomach.

Jesse held on for dear life as they took off. The journey started slow, as they still had to get through the mayhem of the street. When the number of people dwindled, the driver let loose.

The sickening rollercoaster ride of the sharp turns and narrow misses made Jesse fear for his life. He began to wish he had a helmet, but that was a fool's wish. His life was now in the hands of the Vietnamese man he'd just met.

Fear prevented Jesse from tracking the length of the journey, but before long, the scooter was pulling off the side of the road.

The dark jungle loomed ominously on both sides of the highway. This place was absent of even the merest flicker of a street light, indicating they were now well clear of the city.

"You are out of Hanoi," the driver stated proudly, leafing through the Greek's money. He split the bundle in half and gave it to the other driver. "You're on your own now, though."

Jesse privately thought the scooter driver's total disregard for their well-being was almost admirable. It was comical to the extent it was bordering on absurdity. He'd just dropped some strangers off in the middle of nowhere and couldn't give a damn.

Without another word, they turned around and sped off, leaving Jesse and the Greek with nothing but each other and the darkness.

"Well, this is just great," the Greek moaned, looking blankly at the wall of vegetation that confronted them.

"We will move off the road and find a clearing to sleep in. Hopefully, we can start a fire," Jesse offered optimistically.

The Greek gave Jesse a reproachful look but didn't suggest an alternative plan.

As they pushed through the gloom, stumbling over roots and feeling the slaps of the foliage, the Greek dropped his tirade of complaints to focus on not tripping.

If a small dirt clearing hadn't quickly emerged, Jesse would've been tempted to give up. The all-consuming blackness of the forest mirrored his optimism. How was this his life? He'd been a cop. It was an ordinary job for an ordinary man. He'd seen a monster, been put on stress leave, been kidnapped by foreign agents, tied up and beaten for days, escaped and killed a werewolf, fled overseas, and now here he was, traipsing blindly through the jungle...

When, at last, he saw the night sky above, Jesse wanted to collapse into a heap and sob. If the Greek hadn't been with him, there was a good chance he would've done just that. Pride was a powerful tool in that moment; it was the only thing keeping him going.

The Greek proved himself useful when he managed to start a fire. It took several long minutes of him fumbling in the dark with a flint striker he'd pulled from his clothes.

Sitting on the damp grass, bathed in the orange glow of the dancing flames, the two men finally had the opportunity to talk properly. The Greek wasn't waiting to judge Jesse's mood before he launched into another verbal assault.

"So, this is your best course of action? To hide in peasant fields and forests of this country," he spat.

"I need to think," Jesse retorted, his voice equally venomous.

"Dragan Cudoviste is dead. You are his natural successor. As I have already tried to explain, there is only one place for you now. Return with me to Vatican City and see your affliction embraced by the Church."

Jesse frowned. "The scar-faced man, this Dragan; he was insane. That whole time you had me imprisoned underground, he was muttering religious dogma and laughing. That is not my future."

"Dragan came from a difficult background. The Church gave him purpose and made him a weapon, but that is irrelevant to you. Bearers of the full moon curse are always cut from different cloths. You do not need to be what he was. You are cursed! But in that curse are gifts... gifts from the old gods."

26

"Gods," Jesse muttered, shaking his head. A log collapsed into the fire, releasing a brilliant cascade of sparks. The fire glowed in the Greek's beady eyes as he stared at Jesse.

"The Vatican pretends there is only one god, their god. But they know it is a lie. You will learn the secret histories of gods and monsters while you come to understand your gifts."

"And why are you so eager for me to go to the Vatican?" Jesse shot at the Greek. "I'll tell you why. You wanted to kill Josh and failed. Not only that, the Vatican's pet monster was killed by me! You want to take me as a replacement to cover up your failings."

There was no hint of a lie in the Greek's eyes as he spoke, "You are right. My failure will be met with harsh punishment. This, however, should have no bearing on your decision, as you have no other sensible options. In a month, you will become the same monster he was. Do you wish to kill the innocent because you were too arrogant to see the correct path forward?"

"No," Jesse answered reluctantly. He ran his hands through his hair as he contemplated other ideas. His mind couldn't conjure anything that seemed like a plausible alternative.

"My name is Vasiliki," the Greek got up and offered his hand to Jesse.

Jesse's mind was still reaching for a better idea. Anything would do.

"They won't lock me up, will they?" Jesse asked Vasiliki. He was aware the question sounded pathetic, but it needed to be asked.

"Quite the opposite. The Vatican will unlock you. A better man will be born beneath the full moon. A man guided by the

27

holy light of the Church. Your work will be honourable. You will be crafted into a weapon, not a test subject."

Jesse was so tired that he couldn't process Vasiliki's sales pitch. All that mattered was that the Vatican understood his new affliction. It was the one place he wouldn't become a test subject in a lab. To Jesse, that was a fate worse than death; that was being pressed against iron bars in the torrent again.

"I'm not agreeing to anything," Jesse began, standing up and grasping Vasiliki's hand. "But I will come to the Vatican with you."

Vasiliki grinned broadly, the firelight distorting his features horrifically. For a moment, he took on the visage of a demented clown with a large moustache.

A branch snapped.

Jesse spun as Vasiliki grunted in alarm.

He could smell something. He could smell people... all around. The conversation had made him oblivious to the approaching danger.

"We need to go," Jesse whispered through gritted teeth as he quickly began stamping out the fire.

As if his words were a summons, men emerged from the undergrowth all around them. They were completely encircled.

Torchlight shined right into Jesse's eyes, obscuring his view of the strangers.

Vasiliki swore loudly in Greek and raised his hands.

"Identify yourselves!" Jesse demanded.

There was a hard whack as something collided with the back of Jesse's head.

CHAPTER THREE   SLAVE

J esse groaned as he stretched. There was a stifled, annoyed grunt as Jesse's hand gently hit the face of the sleeping man in the bunk next to his.

Jesse didn't even bother to apologise. He didn't care for the other slave workers in the compound and they didn't care for him. They figured because he was a Western man, he'd eventually be rescued, while they had no way out of this hell.

By Jesse's best estimation, he'd been in the drug runner's compound for almost a month. He'd awoken in the back of a vehicle beside Vasiliki, bound in heavy chains and gagged. They'd travelled for hours through the ceaseless green of the jungle. To make things worse, once they'd come to the edge of a large river, Jesse had been blindfolded and knocked out again.

The compound he now called home was old, decrepit and powered by large generators that frequently failed. Not that power ever made it to the slave quarters.

Armed guards frequently patrolled the perimeter. Jesse had counted at least thirty, though noticed new faces would periodically emerge among their ranks.

It wasn't a guess that drugs were being manufactured here; Jesse had seen what was being loaded into the trucks that were driven away in the dead of night. And it wasn't only common narcotics being trafficked. There were several large warehouses that Jesse hadn't been allowed access to that seemed wholly unrelated to the compound's primary business. There was also an out-of-place colonial-style mansion that served as the home for the bosses, shadowy figures Jesse hadn't yet laid eyes on. There were no modern facilities. Toilets consisted of a row of abhorrent long drops, while bathing was restricted to jumping into a nearby stream under the watch of half a dozen guards. Due to Jesse's sheer size, he could never get in or out of the small toilet sheds without getting some loose faecal matter stuck to his clothes.

Sickness ran rampant through the camp as mosquito-borne diseases wreaked havoc. There was no netting for protection as the evening swarm descended.

Jesse was in hell.

He'd run through scenario after scenario as to how he could get away, always finding an impediment to his plans. He'd drawn rudimentary sketches in the dirt and stolen what loose objects he could, but it was all futile. The key ingredient he'd needed over the last month was luck, and it was in short supply.

This was a big operation, so the drug runners had clearly planned for potential problems. Fighting wasn't an option, as Jesse was weak from hunger. They were kept on the point of perpetual starvation, only offered runny oats and discarded fruit when the guards allowed it.

The walls were tall and thick, topped with razor wire, and

the main doors were lit with bright spotlights and guarded by a mounted machine gun. Save for a miracle, Jesse wasn't getting out that way.

Jesse committed as much detail about the daily running of the compound to memory as he could. Such a vast operation had to have flaws to be exploited and weak links in its proverbial chain.

It wasn't just the drug operation Jesse had memorised. Exotic animals were trafficked or killed for their pelts, while boxes of military-grade explosives were moved in and out. These criminals had a diverse portfolio of illicit activities.

The nearest thing Jesse had to a friend in this place was Vasiliki, and they were far from close. Jesse's obvious dislike of the man had led him to abandon using his name. It humanised the Greek, and Jesse didn't view him as human. By god, did he hate that man. He was the monster that had led Jesse to this awful place.

Similarly, the Greek blamed Jesse for their capture and the current situation. Jesse admitted to himself that the Greek wasn't entirely wrong, yet still did not feel entirely to blame. These were circumstances beyond his control.

Jesse gazed up at the roof from his top bunk. The rusted sheet metal meant to keep them dry had been haphazardly placed, meaning water rolled in through small holes and fell into the shelter in small streams. At first, Jesse had found being perpetually doused as he tried to sleep a frustration beyond comprehension, but now it didn't bother him. He could feel himself growing bitter and resentful. He lay there, feeling the ceaseless drips on his scalp, wallowing in his misery.

An obnoxious gong rang outside. It was struck three times, signalling the beginning of the work day. Along with the twenty other people who called the dilapidated shack home, Jesse shuffled out of bed and pulled on his dirty overalls. Rats darted around the weary men's feet as they made for the door.

Jesse pulled it open and was hit with the smells of the rainforest. There were other smells here too: machinery, cement and diesel. He didn't like it.

A small man with a big gun began barking orders in Vietnamese. Since Jesse didn't understand, he was usually escorted to his designated workplace for the day. Sometimes he was hauling boxes and sometimes he was packing unknown substances into boxes. Then, occasionally, it was construction work. Construction work was the worst, as the guards were the cruellest. There was no way to fight back. He'd seen several men executed for daring to speak up for themselves.

Jesse hadn't bothered to mention the werewolf curse, and not just because he'd never be believed. The people who ran this place deserved a fate worse than the justice system could devise. They exported their misery to the world, taking advantage of the weak and stupid. Soon enough, Jesse would be the instrument of his vengeance. The grim satisfaction he took in this thought kept him going. The Greek, however, vehemently disagreed with this approach.

A hunched figure bumped into Jesse. Hell enjoyed summoning demons for his torment and had done so again this morning. It was the Greek who'd appeared.

"Almost a month, we have been here," he mumbled.

The Greek looked like a shell of his former self. He'd lost considerable weight and was noticeably shaggier. He always had a haunted look about him that Jesse found amusing. After all, this was the man who'd held him hostage and beaten him. Karma had come quickly, though unfortunately, it'd caught Jesse in its wide net.

Jesse didn't say anything.

"The full moon will be tonight," the Greek whispered hoarsely.

Jesse shrugged.

"You cannot be so cavalier with our lives! With my life!" the Greek murmured, almost pleading.

"What can I do?" Jesse shot back at him.

"Attack a guard," the Greek suggested.

"They will kill me."

"They may lock you up in a more secure prison."

"I am not going to die to save you," Jesse stated absolutely. For a moment, he heard the bitterness in his own voice.

"Why not?" the Greek spat back. "Your life is pointless anyway. You were handed a gift from the gods and instead of taking good advice, squandered it! You are pathetic."

Rage flashed in Jesse's mind. He grabbed the Greek by the overalls and flung him to the ground. A second later, Jesse's fist connected with the Greek's nose.

A guard shouted at them in Vietnamese, then Jesse was roughly pulled off his squirming foe. He was led away from the crowd and towards a small concrete building.

"What new nightmare is this?" Jesse sighed internally.

A trio of men emerged from the building, the leader sizing Jesse up.

"Big strong man," he said in broken English, his gleeful tone impossible to miss.

Jesse scowled. His offensive gesture was noticed, causing one of the guards to hit Jesse in the back with the butt of his rifle.

"Strip him."

One guard pointed his rifle at Jesse's face, while the other unclipped his uniform, then tore off his shirt.

It took all of Jesse's power not to fight back. And damn did he want to fight. Sweat dripped from his forehead as his clenched fists trembled with rage. The muzzle of the rifle, with its gleaming cold steel, forced Jesse to remember that he didn't want to throw his life away pointlessly.

The leader stepped back through the door and quickly re-emerged with a weapon and an ecstatic grin. At three feet long, it was a plaited leather rope with nine thin thongs dangling from its end. Each of the thongs was knotted several times.

Jesse gulped. He knew this tool. It was a sadistic torture device known as the Cat-O-Nine-Tails. He was going to be whipped.

The guards kicked out the back of Jesse's knees, causing him to collapse into the mud. He was swiftly forced into a kneel, then leaned forward in a macabre imitation of prayer. Jesse knew all too well that no gods were listening to the prayers of the damned in this place.

As if by divine timing, the monsoonal downpour began. Jesse felt each cold drop as the ground turned into a brown slosh around him.

Jesse's hands were bound behind his back as a gag was pushed into his mouth. He choked and spluttered, causing the guards to laugh. It was a cruel, mirthless laugh that the concrete walls amplified.

He could feel the rope strangling his wrists. It itched and scratched while the taste of the soiled cloth in his mouth made him want to vomit.

Jesse buried his discomfort in a vain attempt at maintaining his dignity. The worst was still to come.

He tried to brace, but nothing could've prepared him for the overwhelming sensation that consumed him moments later.

The pain was surreal.

The nine knotted thongs of the whip cut through his skin with extreme prejudice. Jesse doubled over, unable to breathe. His entire back seized up as fire shot through every nerve. It was incomprehensible. It was blinding. The mud was quickly mingled red with blood.

Seeing nothing but white, Jesse struggled to inhale through his nostrils.

The whip struck again, and Jesse collapsed.

The guards righted him, and the process repeated. Over and over. The repetition did little to dull the impact of the whip. Its biting sting only intensified with each hit.

As the whip shattered his body, Jesse longed for the cold embrace of death. It was better than this. Anything was better than this.

Yet, all he could do was scream into his gag until even his

voice left him.

He could barely comprehend the annoyed voices of the men around him. They seemed perplexed by something, though Jesse couldn't understand what as he was almost delirious with pain.

Winded and trembling, Jesse was lifted back to his feet.

"You heal!" the leader shouted at Jesse, his voice a curious mix of confusion and annoyance.

In his daze, Jesse groggily nodded, hoping for the ordeal to be over. He had no idea what the man meant and didn't care to understand.

Looking disgusted, the leader spat in Jesse's face. He then issued further orders, and Jesse was dragged away.

As was customary, Jesse was given no time to recover from his vicious beating. Instead, he was sent to an area of the compound he hadn't been to before. He found himself beside the 'forbidden warehouses', or so he'd labelled them in his head. Jesse didn't even know if they were off-limits, or if they just preferred him to work in other areas of the compound.

Much to his surprise, the pain of his punishment didn't last. After fifteen minutes, Jesse was fine, as if he'd never felt the brutal lash of the whip.

"How can that be possible?" Jesse considered.

He had, however, become aware that he felt incredibly seasick. His stomach was churning something fierce, growing in intensity as the seconds passed.

He didn't have time to ponder this new conundrum. A guard pointed him towards a pallet laden with boxes. This man was half Jesse's size with a thin moustache and terribly crooked teeth.

36

He had zero English ability, but Jesse didn't need an explanation. Apparently, he was to join the throng of malnourished men unloading the boxes and carrying them uphill to a series of waiting flatbed trucks.

At least today's work was simple.

• • • • •

HOURS PASSED BENEATH the periodic rainstorm until something broke the monotony of the task. Noise appeared in the distance... like a familiar sound from another life. It was a far-off buzzing or whirring... an aircraft of some kind... a helicopter!

Two sleek silver choppers appeared on the far horizon. They were coming in fast. As the unfamiliar vehicles zoomed overhead, Jesse could make out the logo on each side.

"iHeal Genetics," Jesse murmured, perplexed as to why such a prominent and well-known company would send emissaries to this seedy place.

The helicopters were deafeningly loud as they skimmed the treetops, disappearing behind the canopy.

They hadn't gone far as Jesse could still hear the rotors whirring. He focused on the sound and tried to estimate the distance to the landing area. It couldn't be more than a couple of hundred metres away.

Once the noise had dimmed, the irritated-looking guard began shuffling the workers through a large metal roller door away from the pallets of unmarked boxes.

Jesse deliberately moved as slowly as possible. It was worth risking another beating in the hope of catching a glimpse of whoever was approaching.

He got lucky.

Right before the roller door to the southernmost warehouse was lowered, Jesse saw a cluster of people emerge from the tree line. The group was fronted by armed guards in black uniforms. These weren't drug runners.

The well-equipped mercenaries were escorting a tall woman with long black hair in a neat ponytail and a formidable-looking man with white hair and a square jaw. The pair looked European.

The guard shouted at Jesse and shoved him through the roller door. He grew instantly frustrated. Maybe if these strangers saw him, they'd know he didn't belong. Maybe they'd rescue him...

No, that was foolish. They were here to deal with the scum that occupied this compound. If anything, they were probably more dangerous than the Vietnamese criminals.

The guard, unsure what to do with his workers, began directing them to random places to carry out menial tasks.

Jesse was given a grimy cloth and spray bottle and then asked to clean. To clean what exactly, he didn't know.

Finding himself temporarily unsupervised, Jesse stole away into a series of small offices lining the side of the main production area. He wanted to see where the strangers had gone. The wild idea of following the path to the helicopters had occurred to him, but he was sure they'd be guarded.

Jesse came to a dark stairwell. He figured that if he couldn't get out, he might as well go up. He walked as quietly as he could to a second-floor landing and cursed when he observed the lack of windows.

There were more offices here and they looked well-used. Jesse's police sense told him that this place was important and that he probably shouldn't be here, which was perfect! There were binders positively overflowing with documents and computers, too! If there was internet, then he could contact the outside world. Finally, Jesse's desire to obtain knowledge about the inner workings of the compound had come to fruition.

He scrambled to the nearest terminal and pushed the on button. What he discovered on the monitor was an operating system he'd never seen before. To make matters worse, the fluorescent green writing blinking on the screen was entirely in Vietnamese.

Jesse cursed himself for allowing a brief spark of hope to manifest in him.

He moved into the next office and found a crudely drawn map on the desk. The compound was clearly visible in the centre. Some distance to the north was a small jetty circled in red. There was also a time and date noted.

A delivery, perhaps? Or maybe something was being smuggled out along the river...

Jesse scanned the room for a calendar and found one pinned to a corkboard beside the door. Each preceding day had a shining red cross through it, meaning he'd discovered today's date. The river delivery was four days from now.

This felt like a wildly important discovery despite his still not having an adequate escape plan.

A female voice carried down the hall, causing Jesse to duck

beneath a desk.

Oddly, the woman was speaking perfect English. It had to be the lady from the helicopter. They'd come here, meaning the guard, in his haste, had potentially shuffled the slaves into the wrong warehouse. The spark of hope suddenly flared into a small flame.

Jesse could hear the clomps of boots as a small group strode into one of the offices down the main hall.

Jesse crawled forward, careful not to raise his head above the desk line. With stealth that didn't suit his bulk, Jesse crossed the divide until he was as close as he could get to the party without inviting his discovery.

Yes! He could hear them clearly now!

The burly, square-jawed man spoke in a very matter-of-fact tone, "Can you fill the order or not?"

Another man, Vietnamese, Jesse guessed, based on his accent, responded in crisp English, "Yes. This is not our usual business, though. It will take time to acquire, then move, these materials."

Jesse poked his eyes up like a crocodile breaching the surface of a waterway.

"And you are certain that your associates won't be suspicious?"

"Mr Napier, please. This is the largest drugs and explosives manufacturing plant in Southeast Asia. No substances will raise eyebrows here, as I am sure you knew when you requested our business."

The man, Napier, grunted his satisfaction with the answer.

"Where are we directing the shipment?" the Vietnamese man asked.

"Siberia. Details will be forthcoming when you have what we've requested."

"And, if you don't mind me asking, what do you want with such an array of bizarre chemicals and rare earth metals?"

The woman replied as she scanned the room with a look of casual disinterest. "Cutting-edge research. Science that is almost magic. In theory of course. Right now, we are in a preparatory phase."

"And Molochtech can't acquire these items through more legitimate measures?"

Napier glared at him, "Of course we could. But we don't want any of our business tracked. Why else would we be here? In this godforsaken jungle? This isn't my idea of a holiday destination. Is it yours, Mia?"

The woman, Mia, looked at the Vietnamese guide with a sudden gleam of interest in her eyes. "Tell me something. I have heard that the Australian Government has specialist forces scouring the Vietnamese countryside. Why would that be?"

The guide just looked at her blankly.

This, however, greatly piqued Jesse's interest. Sager and the AST were still looking for him! They were clever and resourceful. No matter how well hidden this compound was, nor how complicit the government was in hiding it, he was sure Sager would find it. After being a slave for a month, becoming Sager's prisoner had now become the preferable option. Though it still wasn't desirable.

"Curious rumours coming out of Australia recently. Hard to know what to take stock in, of course," Mia continued. "I hoped you might know, but it seems not."

The guide shrugged and stated, "If what you're saying is true, we will ramp up our security as a precaution."

"See that you do," Napier stated coldly. "Our boss hates interruptions. He has clients to keep happy, and he prefers to do it in a timely manner."

"Your boss being?" the Vietnamese man asked impertinently.

"Never you mind," Napier grunted.

Jesse watched Mia scan the office with a unique mix of curiosity and mild disinterest etched on her features. She was rake-thin with a long angular face and a high brow. The man, Napier, was the opposite, solidly built with eyes that carried the shadow of atrocities in their depths.

"I think this enterprise will suit us nicely. If Markovic can fulfil his promise to deliver us the wonders he has discovered, our work can begin in earnest in the coming months. So much to do, so much to obtain..." Mia trailed off.

"You have said too much. Mia, come," Napier snarled, annoyed by his colleague's flippant remarks.

The Vietnamese guide directed the pair down the hall.

They strode out of sight, leaving Jesse befuddled. Very little of that had been useful. Still, he was now armed with knowledge of the coming arrival down the river and that the AST were still here. If the stars aligned, there was a chance he could escape this place.

In all the excitement of his eavesdropping, Jesse felt like he had forgotten something important. But for the life of him, couldn't remember what it was.

It was fortunate that the conversation had ended there, as the sound of torrential bucketing rain soon filled the building. The obnoxious chorus of slamming raindrops on the metal roof drowned out the possibility of hearing anything further.

He retraced his steps and returned to the first floor, just in time to be noticed by the harassed-looking guard. The small man shouted at Jesse, directing him out of the warehouse and into the downpour.

For the rest of the afternoon, the rain ignored the slave worker's pleas for it to dissipate and remained an unwelcome guest. As night drew its dark curtain across the forest, the clouds finally broke and unanimous sighs of relief were heard from guard and slave alike.

Jesse was met with an unpleasant surprise. The man who'd whipped him in the morning was approaching, flanked by armed guards. He could only assume that his wanderings in the warehouse had been reported, and he was due another punishment.

The leader barked something in Vietnamese, and Jesse was promptly escorted away from the rest of the group.

Jesse was marched towards the slave quarters, or so he had assumed.

The guards pivoted, and Jesse was turned away from the bunks towards the toilet block.

Knowing better than to ask, Jesse went with them silently.

When the first glimmer of starlight reached out over the trees, Jesse remembered the important thing he'd forgotten.

The full moon was coming! The horror of this day wasn't over yet. It was only beginning...

A peculiar locked shed sat at the end of the row of stinking long drops.

The lead guard pulled a key from around his neck and opened the door.

A putrid stench flooded Jesse's nostrils. Even in the dim light, he could see that this was another toilet, though a particularly filthy one. Excrement was bubbling through the top of the hole, indicating it was beyond full. The internal walls and roof were also equally coated with the brown substance, as if someone had decided, upon seeing the overworked bowl, to spray the rest of the area with their waste instead.

Barely visible among the excrement were thick chains with solid clasps on them. Jesse's punishment for his disorderly conduct wasn't over yet.

Under the watch of the guards, Jesse stripped off his mud-soaked clothes and presented for inspection. Satisfied there was no way Jesse could escape, he was shoved inside. One guard gingerly worked to fix the clasps to Jesse's wrists, swearing as he brushed against the walls.

Once Jesse was secured, he left.

With a bang and clunk, the door was locked. Standing completely naked with his toes sinking into the faeces, in total darkness, Jesse whimpered.

Due to the hard day's labour, most of the workers would've fallen asleep instantly. Jesse had no such luxury. There would be no sleep tonight. He wouldn't even sit down in this horrid room.

Jesse pulled hard against the chains binding his wrists, but they didn't budge. He was so weak and so dreadfully tired.

His feeling of seasickness hadn't abated.

He was angry. He'd never been this angry in his life. But then, in this moment, his life had never been worse.

Much like the bunk room, the toilet shack had a flimsy roof laced with holes. Through them, Jesse could see the black of the night sky. There were no stars here, just the dark void above.

It was coming.

The change.

Jesse wondered how long it would take.

Was the full moon sitting there in the night sky right now?

Through the small gap in the roof, Jesse saw a white glimmer pierce the black canvas above.

The world became fire.

CHAPTER FOUR DEATH

Something thin and wet slapped Jesse in the face, waking him from his dreamless sleep. With a groan of disgust, he extracted himself from the thick, gooey mud that had evidently been his bed and blinked several times in quick succession.

Total confusion overwhelmed him.

"Where am I? What the hell..."

Memory returned in slow drips. He was in Vietnam. He was a prisoner of the drug runners! Or, he was...

Jesse got to his feet and scanned his environment.

The sun was high in the sky, though heavily obscured by the dense canopy. It was clearly around midday. Gone were the dreary walls and rusted metal roofs of the compound. Instead, a spectacular jungle now engulfed him. There were no clear indications of a track, though there was something else.

Large clawed footprints cut out swathes of mud in his immediate vicinity. They were unlike the footprints of any animal Jesse knew of. Even more worrying was that they stopped right where he now stood.

Jesse literally slapped some sense into himself and quickly realised two things. Number one was that he was completely naked. Number two was that every muscle in his body burned with a furious intensity like he'd never experienced. This could only mean one thing.

It had happened.

Last night, Jesse Billiau had become a monster.

Jesse scrambled to his feet, his aching bones protesting all sudden movement. He ran his hands across his torso. Where just yesterday he'd been wretchedly skinny, a result of his month of near starvation, he was now incredibly lean and muscular. It was as if he'd never missed a meal. Jesse ogled his new spectacular physique in awe.

Then, alarm gripped Jesse as a devastating worry wrapped his mind like an enormous coiling serpent.

"Okay, I transformed," Jesse stuttered. "I know that much. I transformed and ended up out here. I escaped the compound, so that's a plus."

But then, Jesse considered the implications of that fact. He knew the compound was remote. So, he must now be even more remote, lost in the wilderness of Vietnam. He couldn't set off into the wilds by himself, could he?

No. Jesse needed direction. He needed resources. How could he get them?

He had no memory of last night. He'd suspected that the monster inside of him wouldn't share his mind, and this all but confirmed it. What he'd become beneath the full moon was its own creature, and its adventures were not stored inside Jesse.

Only one solution made sense, though he didn't like it. While the tracks were fresh, Jesse could follow them back to the compound. He could then survey the facility and make a plan. In the dead of night, he could strike.

Perhaps the werewolf had caused so much chaos and stirred so much fear in the guards that they had fled the place. That was the most optimistic result he could hope for. Then again, the appearance of a monster may have caused them to lock it down and fortify it...

It didn't matter. Jesse was confident he could scout the compound without being detected. Some information was better than no information.

Jesse picked a crawling insect from his upper thigh. He didn't particularly like being completely naked in a forest full of creatures that could sting and bite. Briefly considering the idea of making underwear out of leaves, then writing it off as absurd, Jesse began his long march through the green in nothing but his skin.

The wave of sickness that had engulfed him yesterday was gone. While incredibly sore, he found he could move easily. He only paused to pull leeches from places where there shouldn't be leeches. His senses were far more attuned. Animals that moved like swift shadows in the undergrowth couldn't avoid Jesse's superhuman sight, smell and hearing. He could feel the presence of lurking beasts watching him from a distance like a sixth sense, so he armed himself with a large stick. Even without the weapon, he felt strong and fast, like no challenge was insurmountable.

No trouble found Jesse as the slow hours of walking passed.

The muddy path was a reliable guide. Even when he lost it in dense vegetation or across streams, it quickly reemerged after some detailed searching. He thanked his lucky stars that rain hadn't arrived to wash away the trail as the clouds above looked ready to burst and release another torrent on the forest.

In the late afternoon, as the sun hung low over the canopy, the trees parted as a rough road emerged.

At long last, he'd found a sign of the compound. He was amazed at how far he'd travelled from it. And why? Had the beast been chased away in a hail of rifle fire? Would there be heightened security searching the undergrowth for a hideous wolfman, in case it came back?

Jesse paused, straining his ears. There was the distant grumbling and spluttering of the generators but nothing else. No vehicles were moving, and no people were speaking.

The wind began building as the grey storm clouds arrived to blot out the sun.

Jesse smiled, which was unusual. The weather had been his second-most hated enemy for a month, but now the building monsoonal storm would be the perfect cover for his approach.

Using caution as his guide, Jesse stuck to the undergrowth as he moved down the road. Like a big metal eyesore, the thick steel fence surrounding the outer compound rose from the brush to signal to Jesse that he'd made it.

While Jesse had never seen the gates, as they were hidden from view by the solid outer walls, he was still surprised to see one sitting half-opened, completely unguarded. It looked as if it had been forcibly dragged open.

This wasn't right...

Rain began pouring down from the heavens, growing in intensity so quickly that Jesse was drenched in seconds.

A distinct fuel odour crossed Jesse's nostrils. He looked across the road and saw the wreck of a Chinese-made BearCat.

Even through the blur of the rain, he didn't have to investigate to know what had happened. The metal was ripped in such a way it was as if powerful claws had dug through the sides. The windscreen had been smashed in from the outside, and only now was the rain washing away the blood. The driver had been pulled out by a monster...

A strange feeling arose in Jesse's stomach, like a tumbling mix of fear and guilt. He found himself pausing to consider if he should press forward. Did he want to know what had happened here last night?

"No," Jesse told himself. "I need to see."

Abandoning stealth, Jesse crossed the divide between forest and compound.

As he advanced, he noticed the mud beneath his feet was tinged red. He passed beneath a guard tower and through another smaller gate into the forward compound. He saw the distant warehouses and the colonial mansion through the trees. To his right were the slave quarters and the stinking row of toilets.

Carnage was everywhere.

Bodies were splayed in the dirt all around.

Necks were torn open and innards were spilled in gruesome fashion. Hands, legs and arms, cleanly torn from their owners, were scattered so randomly and thoroughly they could've passed for abstract art.

It was clear that the slaves had been trying to run. The monster had jumped from person to person, ripping them to pieces.

Jesse threw up, the steaming filth splashing across his feet.

Had he done this?

He walked forward in a daze, the rain pounding on his skull like the beat of an incessant drum, a drum heralding a rising tide of guilt like he'd never felt. This was horror beyond words, beyond what a human mind should be capable of conceiving.

Jesse ran, wanting to escape the scene, yet stumbled when he slipped in a slimy pile of intestines and stomach fat. Jesse looked down to see the empty eyes of the Greek staring up at him. The echoes of terror remained in the man's vacant orbs.

Despite all the ill will Jesse had wished his captor, he would trade his life to undo the act of supreme savagery that had occurred.

The mud sloshed beneath him as Jesse followed the familiar paths of his daily chores, pressing forward like a zombie.

The bodies became that of the guards. Spent casings littered the ground, indicating that they'd put up a hell of a fight.

As he approached the colonial-style mansion, Jesse saw more bodies hanging from the windows.

Even here, guard and worker alike lay in the muck, torn to bloody pieces. The werewolf had been everywhere, and it had killed everyone.

Hopelessness overwhelmed Jesse.

It was one thing to wish ill will upon evil people, but to see his

FEAR THE FULL MOON

prayers answered in such a way... Had this been what he wanted? How could he now live knowing what he'd done? He'd come here to escape a cage and now found himself behind bars from which he could never escape... the bars of culpability for murder that were now reinforced in his mind.

Jesse knelt in the muck, letting the torrential rain wash over him.

"What have I become?" he asked the roaring wind. The gale answered him by shaking the flimsy buildings.

It felt like nature itself wanted to tear this place down to forget the horror that had occurred here.

Jesse looked at the body of the nearest guardsman through his tear-soaked eyes. Still held in the man's lifeless grip was a pistol.

Jesse clambered through the mud towards the corpse and ripped the gun from the unmoving hand.

He contemplated it for a long moment, considering his life and what he'd become. What was his future now? With a simple trigger pull he could rid the world of another monster.

"Tut, tut, tut," an unfamiliar voice cut through Jesse's thoughts.

Jesse spun wildly.

There was someone else here. Someone was alive!

Then, Jesse saw the man, and his elation was replaced with confusion.

Walking through the rain towards him was a tall, dark-skinned man in bizarre attire. He brandished a cane with an ornate silver skull on top. Despite the wind, rain and slosh, his long purple

52

tailcoat was immaculately dry, as was his top hat. His scarf of purple feathers seemed immune to the monsoonal conditions.

The most concerning item the stranger carried was his face mask, fashioned in the image of a skull, which covered everything except his lower jaw. The wide eye holes of the mask revealed the man's shimmering golden eyes, which bore into Jesse with surprising intensity.

This person was so absurd to behold that Jesse figured he had to be a hallucination. But that wasn't right... He could see the stranger as plainly as he could see the gun in his hands.

"Jesse Billiau, how nice that we should meet again," the man displayed his yellow teeth with an unnerving smile.

"How do you know my name?" Jesse asked, quite sure he'd never met this individual before.

"Of course, how silly of me. I have met you, but you have not met me. Allow me to rectify this most egregious error."

The stranger offered a hand, which Jesse was hesitant to take. He looked at the man's pearl-white gloves with immediate distrust.

Jesse's body suddenly acted without his command. He reached up, grasped the stranger's hand, and allowed himself to be pulled off his knees to his feet.

"Who are you?" Jesse shot at the man, staggering backwards in alarm. He'd just been manipulated by some unknown force like a puppet on strings.

"The name's Baron Samedi. Though I have had many names in my time. Old names for the thing I once was... not the thing I am now. Perhaps you relate? You are, of course, intimately familiar with the notion of being one thing, then being something quite different."

Jesse gulped. This stranger knew what had happened here.

"You know about the werewolf curse? How?"

"I've been watching you since you fled the long arm of the law in your home country. Are you so foolish to assume that you escaped so easily without any outside assistance?"

"It did seem too good to be true..." Jesse said slowly, mulling this revelation over in his mind.

Was this madman a manifestation of Jesse's shattered consciousness? Had the horror of this place broken him?

As Jesse stared into Baron Samedi's golden eyes, he picked up on something almost instinctual.

"You aren't human, are you?" Jesse asked, though it was more of a statement than a question.

"No."

"What are you?"

"A god, my boy. A god of life and death."

Jesse shook his head in disbelief. What did he mean by 'a god'? Werewolves were one thing, but gods... come on.

"No need to dismiss and deride," Samedi smiled, reading Jesse's face. "There are many things beyond your understanding that you will soon be familiar with. Our meeting is just the beginning for you. I see as you contemplate that gun in your hands that perhaps you wish to stride across dimensions to the other side. While normally I welcome such travellers, for you, I must insist that you continue living, a request that goes against my very nature."

The sheer oddity of this man's remarks spurred the fire of defiance in Jesse. He felt like challenging this person. He was not entirely broken and wouldn't suffer a fool to mock him.

"Are you a god from ancient Vietnam or something?"

"No. You would have heard of Voodoo, I'm sure. That is the faith that caused my apotheosis. I was once no more than a slave to a master, as my followers were. A tale for another time..."

"Why are you here?" Jesse knew the man was being deliberately vague, adding confusing, nonsensical terms to the conversation to throw him off guard.

"The destroyer sent me to ensure your escape. And good thing he did. If it weren't for me, they would've got you at your house."

"The destroyer?"

"I cannot tell you the specifics. Just be thankful you have friends in such high places."

"I don't believe any of this," Jesse murmured.

"What you believe is of no concern to me," Samedi grinned. "The question now becomes: where do you go from here?"

A memory suddenly struck Jesse. The map with the meeting point on the river. There'd be people coming down the river in a few days. He had everything he needed here to set up an ambush. There was still a way out of this mess!

Jesse dropped the gun.

"The river is my path forward," he told Samedi absolutely.

"Maybe it is, maybe it is," Samedi responded coyly.

"If you are a god, can you cure the curse inside me?" Jesse asked.

"It is not in my domain. The monster inside you will have to be managed by you."

Jesse's confusion morphed into a tide of anger.

"I don't understand this. What is happening right now? What are you? Tell me the truth!"

"I have not spoken the merest semblance of a lie to you, Jesse Billiau," Baron Samedi frowned, as if he wasn't expecting Jesse to be so obstinate in the face of these strange circumstances.

Jesse snorted with rage. How dare this man in his ridiculous clothes talk down to him.

"I have come here to prevent you from making a regrettable mistake. I have other tasks to attend, though I do wish you and your pet wolf all the best."

"Is that meant to be funny?" Jesse hissed.

"My intent is my own to know and yours to interpret as you see fit."

"Have you appeared here to help me? Because if so, you aren't doing a good job."

"Perhaps it is help I offer, in a small way. You have a difficult path laid before your feet that is easy to stray from. I would see your feet stay true to the destiny before you. But don't get me wrong, the deathly gaze of Baron Samedi will be watching you closely from now on, even if you doubt my presence."

"You claim to be a god, but you won't offer me any real help?" Jesse spat. "Why even appear here then?"

"I am simply here to stay your hand and calm your mind. As you walk towards a greater purpose, so do I. Though I do suspect that outside these lands, when the time comes, some unwanted chains and closed doors may suddenly be opened, if you're very lucky," Samedi winked.

The strange god tapped his long cane in the mud, then vanished.

Jesse stood there, utterly bewildered. His earlier despair was completely gone. If anything, the appearance of the self-proclaimed god had awakened a sudden sense of destiny in him.

Whatever his path beyond Vietnam was, right now, he had to get out of this country. He couldn't stay here, in the rain and muck, feeling sorry for himself. He had all the knowledge and tools he needed readily available in the now deserted compound.

Jesse again surveyed the drenched stinking corpses being swallowed by the mud and shook the regret from his mind. These were events bigger than him, and holding on to the notion of a higher purpose would get him through this.

Jesse made a mental checklist. He needed to get out of the rain and find some clothes. He would bury the dead when the rain abated. Once that ghoulish task was accomplished, he could prepare his ambush. In a few days, a boat was coming down the river...

Haste was Jesse's singular focus as he traversed the quiet compound.

The sky didn't look to offer any reprieve from the ceaseless torrent as Jesse began his grim task. He dug hole after hole, blinded by the wind and thudding drops. The ground didn't give easily, but this didn't deter his lonely figure. Silhouetted beneath the storm the grave digger worked for hours on end. His muscles ached, yet he continued with the determination of a damned man seeking a glimmer of redemptive salvation.

As Jesse patted down the thick layer of earth consuming the Greek, he murmured, "I'm sorry." It was the only person he spoke any words for.

When, at last, every remnant of a person had been collected and buried, Jesse collapsed where he stood. Sleep had been tugging at the corners of his mind for hours, and he finally let it overwhelm him.

Jesse woke to an eerie silence beneath the shining sun. He'd always known this place to have a hum of activity, yet now he was the only person here, standing solitary among the small dirt mounds covering the dead. He found the silence unwelcome.

Jesse sucked in a deep breath full of purpose. He had work to do. As a cop, Jesse had always been organised. Still being probationary, it was expected that he would take on additional work with enthusiasm. 'Playing the game', Jesse called it. To get anywhere in a government organisation, you had to play the game.

Jesse located the areas where he'd loaded boxes and boxes of stolen military-grade explosives in the weeks prior.

"Power source, arming switch, firing switch, detonator," he told himself.

Jesse was no pyromaniac, but as a kid, he'd experimented with rudimentary pipe bombs. He'd also done some basic explosives learning in his police training. His goal was to construct a series of traps designed to distract, but not kill.

As the rain began again, pouring down on the metal roof in a deafening cacophony, Jesse bent over a soldering iron and worked.

He'd found switches galore, along with hundreds of metres of wiring. He concluded that tripwires would be almost invisible in the jungle. While his plans had seemed easy in his head, constructing working circuits proved fraught with danger. Almost blowing his fingers off quickly taught Jesse not to jam a detonator into small amounts of explosives before testing his circuit.

It took the entire day, but he finally fell into a groove with a system that worked. Once he'd armed his circuit, a tripwire would start a reaction that would detonate sticks of an explosive called PE4. Jesse had wrapped each stick of PE4 with detonating cord, which he planned to set in targeted locations around the dock. It was hard to visualise without actually seeing the dock, but he only wanted to make one trip. The longer he stayed here the more he risked affiliates of the drug runners showing up.

He was also concerned with not knowing how much of a bang the PE4 would produce. As its packaging was labelled 'high explosive', he assumed one stick per tripwire was all he needed. His goal was a quick series of explosions all around, disorienting the drug runners and allowing Jesse an opportunity to commandeer their watercraft.

After that, it was anyone's guess. A river would lead to a town, and a town could lead to Jesse's salvation. What would he do then?

Without the Greek, he wasn't going to the Vatican. And it was clear he was too dangerous to live in normal society.

"Problems for later," Jesse murmured as he worked.

· · · · ·

LATE ON THE SECOND DAY, Jesse secured what essential supplies he could in a backpack and loaded his explosive traps in the back of a rusted old four-wheel drive, the keys for which he'd stolen from the belt of a dead man.

He was going north to find the river.

Soon enough, Jesse would be a free man again if everything fell in his favour.

CHAPTER FIVE AMBUSH

The whir of an outboard motor cut through the chorus of the forest like an unwelcome guest knocking at the door to Jesse's mind. Reality returned to him, along with focus and adrenaline. Everything was ready.

He'd found himself temporarily lost, drifting off to faraway places as he listened to the particularly throaty call of a nearby bird. The dream of his former life faded as quickly as it had appeared, leaving Jesse somewhat dazed. He was rather surprised at himself when he discovered he'd barely thought about Kayla over the last couple of days camping in the forest. In fact, he'd hardly remembered her existence during his month-long incarceration in the compound. Clearly, that'd been nothing more than a relationship of convenience for him, which felt oddly shameful to admit. Still, that was the past. The danger of the present grew with each sputtering cough of the approaching motor.

Jesse pulled a pair of binoculars from his rucksack and peered through a perfectly curated gap in the foliage. He was hidden on the far bank from the dock. He'd walked for miles up and down the length of the waterway and hadn't encountered any other structures, meaning this jetty had to be it. He could see one of his tripwires glinting in the light, invisible to all but him. Though none could ever spot Jesse's hiding place, he'd taken every step possible to become a ghost. His exposed skin was coated with thick gooey mud. He wore military-style fatigues he'd found at the compound. Beside him was a fully loaded rifle, partially covered by ferns. Carrying the weapon across the river while preventing it from getting wet had been a challenge Jesse had risen to. He'd wanted it here for overwatch but had no intention of using the gun. This was going to be a mission of stealth and subterfuge.

Being ever-cautious, Jesse had buried a similar pair of weapons near the jetty, though he hoped not to need them. If all went to plan, Jesse would be out of here before anyone noticed his presence.

Jesse peered down the river. He couldn't see the boat yet but was sure it was only minutes away.

Yesterday afternoon, a large drone had come screaming across the forest at a breakneck pace. Jesse had expected pre-arrival scouting to occur, but not in such a technologically advanced way. He'd dived into dense brush as it'd zoomed overhead. Since nothing had followed up its patrol, Jesse remained confident he hadn't been seen.

The sleek black shell of the drone flickered in Jesse's memory, then transformed. A haunting image lingered at the forefront of Jesse's mind. It was a skull mask with brilliant golden eyes beneath it. The hairs stood up on the back of his neck. Was that man, the one who considered himself a god, here? He'd said he'd be watching over Jesse...

"Give me some luck," Jesse murmured, hoping he was talking to more than just himself.

The boat entered Jesse's field of view, slowing as it approached the jetty. It was not well-maintained, with a paint-stripped hull and formidable holes in its side. There were eight men crammed into the small space offered by the vessel. While the boat had a rusted cabin, it looked to be little more than an oversized dingy.

As Jesse suspected, each man had a rifle slung over his shoulder. Yet, they all looked relaxed. Evidently, the news of the nearby massacre hadn't filtered through the forest to the wider criminal network.

Jesse's plan was simple. It relied on his assumption that the vanguard would exit the boat and make their way down the jetty, where they'd hit the first tripwire. This would set off an explosion, drawing (hopefully) all the men into the forest's tangled depths, where further blasts would sow confusion. Jesse, meanwhile, would swim across the river, commandeer the vessel and get away.

Naturally, Jesse had assessed his plan for faults and found dozens, but that didn't matter. He felt strong, fast and powerful. Almost unstoppable. The full moon transformation had re-shaped his body to an exceptional degree, and he would use his profound new fitness to get this done.

Loud voices carried across the wide waterway, cutting Jesse from his thoughts. He didn't need a translator to understand the annoyed utterings of the drug runners. There wasn't a soul present to greet them at their designated meeting point.

A pair of men raised their weapons and cautiously scanned

the environment, suspecting foul play.

A mosquito buzzed past Jesse's binoculars, appearing monstrous as it struggled to find a patch of bare skin on the mud-soaked man. He was too tense to dare even swat at the annoying insect.

Jesse adjusted his bulk as his eyes followed the men moving along the jetty. When they reached the final rotten plank, they hit the taught, near-invisible piece of fishing line suspended between the trees.

BANG!

The explosion carried a brilliant cascade of splinters as an unseen tree was vaporised. Jesse felt the blast in his chest as it careened across the river, its shockwave disrupting the normal flow of air. The stick of military explosive was far more powerful than Jesse had anticipated. It'd thrown both men off the jetty and sent them tumbling down the steep bank of the river.

Confused shouts came from the boat, and all but one of the drug runners ran to assist their comrades. Fortunately, there was no easy way to access the riverbank, meaning the men had to weave into the dense forest. In their haste, the group hit two more tripwires.

The explosions boomed as Jesse's heart raced.

It was now or never.

He crawled forward on his hands and knees, brushing aside the leaves as he slithered down the bank.

With a small splash, he submerged himself in the icy water. He saw the mud exit his skin in droves and float downstream. He cursed his own stupidity. Obviously, the muck would wash away when he swam; how had he not considered this?

Disguises didn't matter now anyway.

He took in a deep sucking breath and dived, moving towards the boat with long powerful strokes.

Another explosion reverberated through the water. The fourth tripwire had been hit.

Despite how he strained to hold his breath, he could not. The length he had to cross was too great for one gulp of air. Jesse had to surface to breathe.

A new sound assaulted his ears.

Gunfire.

There was a firefight happening in the forest. Someone other than the drug runners had arrived... Though, that didn't make sense due to the remoteness of this place. It was either reinforcements from the compound or another group in the vicinity that had been drawn here by the blasts.

Jesse pushed on, diving back into the murky grey of the river. His hand hit the hard outer shell of the vessel, and he rose to draw in another satisfying breath.

The rate of gunfire had increased, and there were more explosions, though not of Jesse's making. Grenades were being thrown. Just what the hell was going on out there?

Jesse pulled himself into the boat, then swore. Despite the chaos, one drug runner remained. His gleaming rifle muzzle was pointed right at Jesse's soaked head.

"BAN LA AI?" he shouted.

Before Jesse could respond, the drug runner exploded in a cacophony of bullets and blood.

Panicked and remembering the horror of the killing field, Jesse stumbled backwards, the entire vessel shifting under his weight.

The undergrowth shook as two men appeared at the end of the jetty, their guns aimed at Jesse. They were wearing military fatigues, but unlike his, theirs were legitimate. They also had bulletproof vests that appeared to be lined with silver...

Jesse had seen similar before, though not here. It was the night that he'd fled Cairns. The AST agents had been wearing body armour lined with silver.

"Get on your stomach! NOW!" one of the soldiers commanded in his distinctly Australian accent.

Jesse just stared at him in bewilderment, contemplating compliance. Somehow, events here had taken a bizarre and inexplicable turn.

More gunfire came from the jungle, causing the two soldiers to dive in alarm. Jesse felt the rush of wind as a bullet escaped the forest and whizzed past his left ear.

There was a sound like a diminished helicopter high overhead. Jesse looked skywards and saw a large black drone hovering about thirty metres above him.

"*AST... the drone hadn't belonged to the drug runners at all, but the AST,*" Jesse thought grimly. They'd found him.

A new face emerged about a dozen metres away and yelled at Jesse. This time, it was one of the Vietnamese criminals, bleeding from a heavy gash on his forehead. Jesse saw the man pluck a small cylindrical object from his belt and toss it into the boat.

After bouncing a couple of times, the object came to rest at

Jesse's feet. He gasped, his feet moving faster than his mind could order the action.

Jesse dived as the grenade exploded, transforming the rear portion of the boat into twisted metal scrap. He tumbled through the grey depths of the river, disoriented and feeling the biting sting of a rib full of shrapnel.

He breached the surface, choking and spluttering. Jesse swam beside the sinking boat and clung to a series of tree roots descending the steep bank.

The firefight in the forest seemed to have intensified, with intermingled Australian and Vietnamese voices springing up between bursts of bullets.

Jesse quickly determined that he had no choice but to head back into the green depths and away from here. With impossible strength, Jesse pulled himself up the bank, the roots threatening to crack at any moment. Still, their stretched sinews held on long enough for him to clamber around a tree and push into the forest.

He quickly came across the bodies of two Vietnamese men left amongst the leaf litter. A shadow shifted nearby, then yet another weapon was pointed in Jesse's face.

It belonged to a skinny, red-haired man in black body armour. He wiped the sweat from his brow and asked, "Jesse Billiau?"

Jesse did nothing. Being confronted with his own name proved to be disorienting. It felt like a lifetime had passed since he'd last heard it.

The man pressed the button on his radio's handset receiver and stated, "Got him, boss. Just east of the jetty."

"Roger. On my way to you."

Jesse knew that voice...

"Turn around and put your hands on your head," the man ordered. Jesse did as he was told, though clumsily. It was as if he'd lost all sense of himself.

"Focus," Jesse thought. Was this what he wanted, to be captured by the Australians after all he'd endured? Of the little he knew right now, he was certain that wasn't a favourable outcome.

If he was just east of the jetty, then that meant that somewhere nearby, attached to a particularly gnarled tree, was a tripwire. With any luck, it hadn't been triggered yet.

The soldier pushed Jesse in the back, forcing him to walk.

Jesse desperately scanned the wall of green for a familiar landmark. Yes! There it was! He saw the tree. His eyes moved to the thin, glinting line coming off its base and stretching to a sapling a few metres away.

Jesse turned and sprinted.

The soldier fired a warning shot into the air, though it was lost amongst the rest of the noise. Jesse knew the man would have no choice but to follow, as the trees were so dense that only a moment of separation could give him the chance to vanish.

Jesse leapt over the wire, his feet displacing the dead leaves around it in a plume of colours and shapes. The soldier didn't mirror his fugitive's jump to his detriment. Another tree-shattering boom ripped through the jungle.

Jesse and the soldier were thrown from their feet as the shockwave ballooned out, though Jesse rolled and was upright quickly. He felt splinters pierce his skin like a thousand knives. He grimaced, though not for long. His body, which had been working to reject the shrapnel from his ribs, quickly set about ejecting the additional shards of wood. It was almost as if Jesse was shrouded by healing magic, making him impervious to permanent damage.

Jesse spun and aimed for the river. There was no time to collect his buried weapons; evading the AST was all that mattered.

He quickly found the jetty, ignoring its creaks as he ran across its mouldy wooden planks.

"Jesse!" a disgruntled voice shouted.

Jesse turned and saw the thin figure of Liam Sager emerge from the forest. A space of only about eight metres separated them.

Sager had a harrowed, fraught look about him like he hadn't had a restful night's sleep in days.

Another tripwire was hit, causing a further explosion to rock the rainforest.

Liam ducked and shielded himself as a hail of wooden shrapnel streamed in his direction.

Jesse looked at his cowering pursuer. Their eyes met. At that moment, Jesse confirmed that no matter how dire his circumstances seemed, he didn't want to be captured. Surrender was not an option.

Liam swore.

Without hesitation, Jesse dived back into the river and swam for his life.

He navigated the steep bank and darted back into the darkness of the forest on the other side.

Jesse grinned. The AST would not get him today.

Still, his escape plan had failed.

"No more," he told himself.

There were remote villages in the countryside where he could seek shelter and food. He knew he couldn't linger in them as the AST had come so close to claiming their prize. Liam would probably double his efforts to find Jesse in the coming days. He had to go where no one could follow and abandon all thoughts of home and civilisation.

His destination was the heart of darkness, and he'd walk towards it willingly.

CHAPTER SIX

GUILT

Long days of desperation quickly became weeks of longing as Jesse wandered the wilderness. As he'd suspected, the villages and towns he came across were not safe havens. The AST had scoured the countryside, anticipating his movements with surprising accuracy.

He learned not to trust the locals he met on the roads and on the seldom-trodden paths, as they all seemed to be on the lookout for him. Whispers reached Jesse that large cash rewards had been offered for information about him. He'd even seen his own face on loose pamphlets like he was a wanted Wild West villain.

Jesse quickly took to stealing food to survive, but after a second close encounter with Liam Sager and his agents, he began avoiding villages altogether. It was by sheer luck alone that he'd escaped.

After meeting the enigmatic Baron Samedi, Jesse was unsure of luck and chance. Had Baron Samedi been a manifestation of his shattered psyche? Had he invented the Baron to cope with the horror he'd inflicted upon the drug traffickers? Or had he been a side effect of the werewolf transformation? It wasn't unreasonable to think that the inner beast could manifest in Jesse's addled mind. He didn't know and preferred not to think about it, though he had little else to occupy his mind.

Jesse stole away into forests and intimately acquainted himself with the rivers and streams. He taught himself to hunt with his bare hands, though was largely unsuccessful at catching anything other than small game. Jesse struggled to start a fire and feared it would attract unwanted attention, so ate meat raw. He felt primal, like he was walking in the shoes of his less-evolved ancestors.

He tried to track the days so he had a rough idea of when the next full moon would occur. As the face of the moon grew fuller in the night sky, Jesse endeavoured to move further from civilisation.

"Let the beast feast on the creatures of the forest," Jesse repeated to himself as a mantra. "Not people, not again."

Then the day came again when fire shot through Jesse's bones as he twisted and contorted. His mind went blank as he was lost to the wolf within. In the gloom of the forest, surrounded by the roars and howls of the night, the monster was born for a second time.

• • • • •

THE SUN BORE DOWN ON JESSE'S SKIN. It took him a long moment to recognise its intensity. This was odd, as the last thing he remembered was being sheltered beneath the dense canopy, gazing into the heavens...

Next, he noticed the annoying buzz of mosquitos all around. The sound filled his ears and penetrated his mind; it was maddening.

He groaned and slapped at the insects blindly. It hurt to move, but why was that?

Jesse opened his eyes and saw a line of ants scuttling past. He was lying in the dirt, facing the base of a simple wooden building. It almost looked primitive in its construction.

"The full moon!" Jesse gasped.

Lethargy and confusion were replaced with desperate intent as Jesse jumped to his feet. Naked as the day he was born, Jesse spun around. He was in the middle of a small village, surrounded by forest.

Bodies were all around. Men, women and children, ready to bloat beneath the blazing sun, lay scattered through the clearing. All of them shared a similar expression: a look of shock, pain and fear. The smell of putrescence infected the air.

It had happened again.

Last month's horror had repeated itself, only much worse.

A pair of girls, not more than seven or eight years old, lay a few yards from him. One's face was so mangled it was unrecognisable. The other's skull had been shattered as if placed in a vice and compressed.

Despair crippled Jesse, filling him with hopelessness. The pit in his stomach quickly became unbearable, like he'd swallowed the weight of the world.

He sank into the muck. A thousand sunrises and sunsets could've passed as he stared into the dirt, only vaguely aware of his body burning beneath the sun.

Was this his just punishment for fleeing from the Australian Government? He'd valued his freedom as greater than the sum of all these lives. A village massacred... children torn apart... He should've let Liam catch him...

How could he go on?

The melodic chirp of an unseen bird roused Jesse from his stupor.

Tears welled in his eyes.

Jesse had always thought it shameful for men to cry, yet now he couldn't help himself. Like a ceaseless rain, the water tumbled from his eyes into the earth below.

He'd tried. He'd truly tried to go as deep and remote into the forsaken jungle as he could, yet the wolf inside him had found its way to victims.

"Your tears are the tears of a man. Your guilt is a man's guilt. Though the actions that caused them are far removed from your conscious mind," a sombre voice stated.

Jesse didn't move. Part of him had expected this. As he had last month, the skull-faced stranger, Baron Samedi, was back.

"Why are you here again?" Jesse croaked through sobs.

"Because I must be," Baron Samedi answered plainly.

Sadness was swiftly replaced with rage.

Jesse stood up with his fist clenched. He stared at the oddly-dressed man with incredulity in his eyes.

"You claim to be a god, yet you won't help me! Why wouldn't you stop this?" Jesse shouted as frustration bubbled his throat.

"In the rest of your life, up until this point, have you known gods to intervene?"

It took a moment for Jesse to digest the response. He just shook his head.

"Because gods do not. I am here now because greater events than you know are transpiring. Events in which you have a role to play. For all your size, strength and perceived authority, you are consumed by weakness. By guilt for things you cannot understand or control. I would not see that weakness prevent your destiny."

Baron Samedi spoke calmly and slowly, though his voice was not pitying. It had clarity and purpose hidden in its deliberate tones. He pointed his skull-topped cane towards the nearest of the huts, one of the few that hadn't been torn to pieces by the werewolf. With a slight popping sound and an unexpected rush of wind, Jesse found himself inside of it.

Instead of kneeling in muck, his knees now felt the hardwood of a solid timber floor.

Jesse was relieved to find no corpses in here, nor even the slightest hint of a fight. It was a small yet powerful thing to be removed from the carnage outside. He noticed a pile of laundry on the floor and immediately began sifting through the clothes to find anything that fit. He was supremely aware of his nakedness, now confined to a large room with Baron Samedi, and didn't like it.

He picked up a rather worn poncho and threw it over his head, after struggling to squeeze on a pair of all-too-short cargo pants.

As soon as he was adequately dressed, Jesse returned to the anger that had swelled in him. He wanted someone to blame for this. Anyone other than himself. Baron Samedi would do.

Baron Samedi peered at Jesse with an unreadable expression as if expecting the coming outburst.

"Why are you here?" Jesse asked for a second time, venom in his voice.

The Baron pointed his cane at the empty table. A large bottle labelled 'Spiced Rum' and two thick cigars appeared. The Baron picked up a cigar and placed it between his teeth. It lit without the presence of a flame.

"Help yourself. These are two indulgences I particularly enjoy," the Baron smiled. "I will be outside, digging holes for the dead."

Again, guilt washed over Jesse. "I will help!" Jesse spluttered.

Baron Samedi shook his head. "Rest and relax, Jesse Billiau. Have a little, or a lot, of rum, and consider your questions carefully."

With a graceful twirl, the Baron walked out of the primitive hut, closing the door behind him. Jesse was intensely curious about what the Baron was doing, yet had no desire to look back on the slaughter outside.

He considered that a fortunate side effect of the Baron's re-appearance was that confusion replaced his feelings of shame and dread. Just what exactly was this tall, dark-skinned, fancifully dressed being? It seemed that he'd have the opportunity to ask questions and wasn't going to waste it.

After fifteen minutes or so had passed, curiosity finally toppled fear in their battle for dominion of Jesse's mind. Jesse strode to the door and flung it open.

He was confronted with a long row of graves, each topped with a cross, dug through the centre of the village. The Baron worked easily, wielding a sturdy black shovel as he dug into the earth. Smoke rings from his cigar rose and dissipated above his tall top hat.

Quite the odd spectacle was taking place at the far side of the graves. A circle of creatures, roosters and goats, though of no type Jesse had ever seen, appeared to be blocking something from view. Each animal was black as the night with golden eyes. One of the ominous goats spotted Jesse and released a small, mournful bleat. It shifted slightly, revealing enough of the hidden object to horrify Jesse. The bodies of the children were laid out side by side.

Jesse almost threw up. He moved to rush back inside but was halted by Baron Samedi.

"Come down, Jesse," the Baron ordered, almost cheerily. "The work is almost complete."

"What are you doing?" Jesse asked, hesitantly walking towards the first of the graves.

The Baron pulled a pair of circular sunglasses from his tailcoat. Jesse noticed that the glasses were broken, as one eye was missing its tinted black lens. Unconcerned, the Baron put them on and looked around, nodding as if satisfied with something Jesse couldn't perceive.

"The dead are with us," the Baron murmured.

This statement only served to terrify Jesse.

"You do not need to fear them," the Baron continued, reading Jesse's mind. "I will take these men and women across the veil, to a place they will linger for a time before they fade. Neither Heaven nor Hell has a claim to any of them."

"What about the children?" Jesse asked, deliberately avoiding looking towards the roosters and goats.

"I walk the paths through life and death with the utmost familiarity, taking humans with me. One companion I will never stand to travel with is a child who has not yet had the opportunity to live a full life. By my blessing, they will rise to life again. I will guide them to safety from afar, and they will have another chance."

"You can resurrect the dead?" Jesse questioned.

Baron Samedi grinned as he puffed on his cigar.

There was a flash of golden light. It was blindingly bright. Jesse had to turn away and shield his eyes as the entire circle of goats and chickens was enveloped by it.

Then, the animals scattered as three small children rose to their feet. The kids appeared confused, rubbing their eyes as if they'd just awoken from a long sleep. Baron Samedi strode towards them, then knelt down.

Jesse assumed the Baron's skull mask would frighten the children, but that wasn't the case. Baron Samedi spoke softly to the children in Vietnamese, with all of them seeming to understand.

The children began walking into the forest, flanked by black roosters and goats.

Baron Samedi turned back towards Jesse. "They will be protected," he stated.

"How did you do that?" Jesse gasped in utter shock.

"I am a god of life and death. A rarity, even among the divine.

I am granted the ability to manipulate life without repercussion from the watchers in the dark, and it is a gift I use to its fullest extent."

"Why not bring them all back?" Jesse asked, a fevered idea springing to the forefront of his mind. The Baron could resurrect the entire village!

"Because that is not how death works. I take pity on the children, because I can. But life is meant to end. Whether by sudden accident or werewolf massacre. When your time arrives, I, or another, will greet you, and you will fade from this world."

"That sounds like an excuse!" Jesse derided, feeling anger bubble up in him again.

Baron Samedi gave Jesse a stern look. A look that he interpreted as 'I am a god and you are not'.

"You can undo what I have done! You can make it right! So, make it right!" Jesse demanded.

"No," the Baron stated. "Go back inside. I will return when the children are safe. Drink the rum; it will calm your mind."

As he ever-so-annoyingly seemed to do so, the Baron vanished into thin air, leaving Jesse arguing with no one.

Perplexed at witnessing a miracle in real time, Jesse concluded that his best course of action was to return to the hut and wait.

• • • • •

AFTER A TIME, THE BARON appeared in the doorway. He sat directly across from Jesse and picked up a mug. He poured from his rum jug until it was full, then filled a second cup for

Jesse. Looking content, the Baron swirled the mug's murky brown contents as he removed his tall top hat and placed it gently on the floor. Then, much to Jesse's surprise, he removed the skull-shaped face mask.

Jesse was taken aback by Baron Samedi's youthful appearance. He had a strong jaw and short-cropped hair. Even without the mask, his eyes still shone with a mysterious golden gleam.

"Drink," the Baron ordered, and Jesse did so. The rum was unlike anything he'd ever tasted. It wasn't like he was swallowing a liquid but more like a vaporous gas flowing from his cup. It was smooth yet burned slightly.

"Made by slaves of the French a long time ago," the Baron hummed as if lost in a memory.

"What are you?" Jesse sighed, feeling as if the thing across from him would never give a clear answer. Wasn't that the way of the supernatural?

"I am, for the time being, your guardian angel. Sent to ensure you don't deviate from the path on which you now walk."

"An angel," Jesse scoffed. "Right."

Baron Samedi raised an eyebrow. "With what you have seen, you would doubt this claim?"

"Angels and gods… its silly…"

"And werewolves aren't?"

Jesse paused and considered this. Doubt at Baron Samedi's claim of being a god had gnawed at him since their initial meeting, and yet the man had clearly resurrected the dead.

"I suppose with all that has happened to me, I shouldn't outright reject your claim of being a god or angel."

"I am change incarnate," the Baron mused as he crossed one leg over the other. "And not in the ways you might think. I am the change from life to death, sure, but more than that. I was once a lesser being. I faced great change, as you do now. What you are does not always determine what you will be."

"I've never believed in destiny," Jesse shrugged.

"Nor should you," the Baron smirked. "It's silly. To wait for fate is a fool's purpose. We make our own destinies."

"But then, all of this was thrust upon me. I didn't choose to be bitten. I didn't choose all this death..."

"And still, here you sit, in a shack in Vietnam, across from the Voodoo Lwa of Death. Extraordinary circumstances."

"What are you?" Jesse asked again, impatience in his voice. He didn't know anything about Voodoo other than it was some kind of satanic religion focused on black magic.

"Voodoo is not satanic, nor is its magic evil," Baron Samedi frowned. "Voodoo is far closer to your traditional religions than you might realise. While you call him God, or Yahweh, or Jehovah, or Allah, we call him Bondye. The supreme god, or the one god."

"How can there be a 'one god' if you claim to also be a god?"

"Humans and their stories have confused things. There were, and are, many gods. When the angels of Heaven spread their war into Africa, many of the old gods fought and perished. Some fled while others bowed to the new regime."

"A war?" Jesse asked. Despite being raised Catholic, he didn't know much about religion.

"Yes, a grand war that smothered the Earth. Angels fought across the world to gain power and influence. It started in the

Roman Empire and then spread."

Baron Samedi paused and stroked his chin, as if considering how best to continue without confusing Jesse.

"Angels are real. As real as your werewolf curse and much deadlier. I was one of them, 1700 years ago, when the war began. I followed my commander into the Underworld with my brothers, and we fell into fire and darkness."

"I don't really follow you," Jesse interjected.

"Do you know what it's like to be lost and hopeless in the absolute darkness of an inescapable pit?" the Baron asked.

Jesse's mind journeyed back to the pounding current of the storm drain. He did, in fact, know the feeling well. He'd carried that fear through his entire adult life.

The Baron smiled knowingly and continued, "It twisted and warped me beyond recognition. You see, Jesse, that is why I am here now. Your mind is weak. You do not seem to grasp that true greatness comes from difficulty and it bothers me. The moment you were bitten, you became uncontrollable death, whether you would want it or not. You cannot control it, or run from it, so you must learn to accept it, as I did."

"I can't see myself accepting this horror... what I've done..."

"It is an old cliche, though it is pertinent for you to understand that without darkness there is no light. From your pain, guilt and suffering, a greater man than you ever could've been will be born, if you simply choose the right path on the forked road before you."

"Have you seen what my life has become?" Jesse croaked, feeling the weight of months of sorrow on his shoulders. "My story isn't a happy one and I can't see a way to change it."

The Baron contemplated this remark for a long moment. "In many ways our stories are mirrored, Jesse Billiau. I will tell you mine, though you may only grasp a little of it as you are woefully ignorant of the higher order of things. Still, you will listen, as in time, it will all make sense."

The Baron took a deep sip of rum. "I was not a god, at first. I was an angel of Heaven. A construct of God designed to be an elite warrior. My name was Samyaza, and I fought under the banner of the Gladius Vaticanus. Our war did not go well."

"What happened?" Jesse asked.

"We ran afoul of an ancient being named Tartarus and were trapped for centuries with no light and no hope. When we were released, I found myself afflicted with malice. An insatiable resentment, like a hunger that couldn't be satiated, consumed me. I became a monster. A demon of the fires of Hell, delighting in the torment of humans. Though I never fell to the levels of pure savagery that dominated my brothers Belial, Astaroth and Asmodee, I was not innocent.

"A day came when Heaven and Hell sealed the unseen paths. Five of my kind, no longer angels but something worse… corrupted creatures we were… were tasked with remaining hidden on the Earth, in service of my old master's will. The Knights of Hell is what we were known as at the time. We were free of the screams of the already tortured souls and let loose on an unsuspecting world. I guided the hands of masters as they tormented their subjects and I set brother against brother in orgies of violence. My hands were not black but red with the blood of humans! Then, she came…"

An almost dreamy look washed across Baron Samedi's face. Jesse knew that look in the way many men did. It was a look of love.

"Mamam Brigitte, hair as red as flame and skin as pale as porcelain, found me. A goddess and beauty like I had never known. She looked past my corruption and helped my eyes, long closed, open again. I saw what I had become. Where once I had purpose, I had become a beast of base instinct. A monster…"

"She wasn't an angel?" Jesse asked.

"No, no… she was from Ireland. An old god of that land who'd been spared by the angels and put into their service. She was a guardian of the past and of heritage. She endeavoured to help the suffering humans, in the ways she could. Brigitte had her own purposes for siding with the angels. Purposes we will discuss in good time, I think…

"It was thanks to her that something miraculous happened. I found a place that belonged to me and a role I was meant to fulfil. I apotheosised. I shed my deformity as a fallen angel and became a god in my own right. Samyaza was a different creature. I became Baron Samedi. With a cast of other surviving gods, we gave our people a new way to worship; something that combined the victory of God with their heritage from the old lands. We let them dance in celebration of the old and new, free of foul purpose. Voodoo was born. The angels did not care about a new religion, so long as prayer was directed in the right place. I was completely severed from my twisted brothers and old master in Hell. The five Knights of Hell became four.

"I know this doesn't mean much to you, Jesse, but it will. Your tale has only just begun. While a monster you may be now, with much suffering to come, you have the potential to rise greater than all those in your lineage. So, drop thoughts of death and release from your current predicament. I will not come to the wails of your despair a third time. Redeem the horrors of the wolf with the actions of the man."

"What should I do?" Jesse asked.

"Isn't that a mighty fine question?" Baron Samedi chuckled. "Go deep into the forests of this land. Run from those who would pursue you. Embrace the pain, the loneliness and the longing, for they will be your only friends in the months ahead."

"To run away from everything... isn't that the opposite of the moral of your story?" Jesse frowned.

"Your critical mind may serve you well in the days to come. You are being hunted, as I'm sure you are aware. To lose your pursuers, you must lose yourself. Shed your identity as a man of the world and embrace the wilds. When the time is right for you to emerge again, I will return to you. You have my word."

Jesse shrugged. Who was he to ignore the advice of a god, if that's what Baron Samedi truly was. Maybe he was a devil in disguise, but even if so, did Jesse not deserve every punishment a devil could deliver?

"Good," Baron Samedi smiled, reading Jesse's mind. "The jungle calls."

Jesse got to his feet and began to run. He didn't know why, but he felt like he should. He bounded out the door, past the graves and into the darkness of the trees.

Baron Samedi's voice rang in his ears as he ran, "The months ahead will be hard. Despite the beast within, you will never truly belong! Fear the beasts of this land and fear the full moon!"

- 2020 -
SOMEWHERE IN SOUTHEAST ASIA...

Jesse was adrift in a sea of memory as he strolled through the sparse broadleaf forest. His eyes swam in the brilliant blue of the sky as he went where his bare feet took him.

The ground was coated in a thick layer of dead leaves that provided satisfying crunches as he stomped on them.

A light breeze ran through the myriad of tall trees surrounding him. Bamboo was becoming more common, which Jesse assumed meant he had travelled far enough for a change in geography.

Where he was, he didn't know. And right now, he didn't particularly care.

Of all the topics that frequently swam across Jesse's mind, today's was monsters. He'd been fortunate enough to come across a stash of old books in a Vietnam war-era structure, all in English. Many had been damaged beyond legibility by the elements, though a good dozen had survived and Jesse had devoured them. In his wild world without a TV or movies, he'd forgotten how engrossing a book could be.

There'd been one large tome dedicated to describing mythological creatures. Naturally, Jesse had dived into it in search of werewolves and learned a lot. The curse indeed came from Greece and had started with a man named Lycaon. He'd also learned that Greek myth held a bizarre array of odd creatures, leaving Jesse wondering how many of them were real. Unfortunately, the book had no mention of gods like Baron Samedi. Still, Jesse found himself reading it front to back, over and over, in the hopes of better understanding the curse that afflicted him. Ironically, he'd decided that in a world of potential monsters, being a werewolf wasn't the worst outcome possible.

He'd left the denser portion of the forest behind as he'd moved steadily downhill, traversing the southern ridge of a canyon.

He admired the beauty out here. The landscape was vast and untouched, with a primordial air about it. The stink and corruption of humanity hadn't touched this wilderness. Life was abundant and rich in its diversity.

Jesse had learned to tolerate his perpetual hunger, as best he could, scavenging when an opportunity presented itself.

Food...

Jesse paused. There was a faint scent being carried in the breeze. It was meat, and it wasn't rotten. There was a dead animal nearby!

Jesse began sprinting like a madman. His inner optimist prayed that a deer had met its untimely end nearby. If he could start a fire, he could feast! A deer could provide several days' worth of food. His clumsy human body, despite being supernaturally enhanced, wasn't suited to hunting such agile prey. Venison would be a real treat.

As Jesse followed his nose, the forest grew sparser. Fields of grass with small yellow flowers greeted the unkempt traveller as he rushed carelessly forward, not concerned with alerting the local wildlife to his presence.

Jesse had come across bears and jackals in his wanderings. He hadn't dared tangle with a bear, but the jackals were skittish and could be frightened away with a stick.

"I hope it's jackals," Jesse prayed as he leapt over a decaying tree.

He pushed through a swathe of green bamboo stalks and emerged by a small clearing.

A deer, quite obviously dead, was lying half submerged in the shadows of the trees not more than a dozen yards away. The leaf litter around it was stained red, and there were clearly injuries to the beast's neck.

Something powerful had killed this animal.

Jesse scanned the clearing, noting its eery stillness. Though, nothing seemed particularly untoward here. There was no movement in the dense brush shielding the forest.

He didn't want to wait for a predator to return for its prize. His impatience directed his actions. Forsaking the cover the environment offered, Jesse strode into the long grass.

As the light of the day bathed his lonely figure, everything changed.

Jesse's pulse quickened. His senses grew instantly sharper as his body responded to an unseen threat. His muscles tensed, ready to fight or flee on his command.

Something was here... something that was used to hiding...

"Show yourself," Jesse growled through gritted teeth.

A much more sinister growl reverberated through the undergrowth in response.

Jesse snapped left and saw the brushes moving. He caught a flash of orange as an obscured figure darted through the shadows.

Then, it was still again. The soothing caress of the breeze returned as if the danger had never been present. Still, the thickets engulfing the sides of the clearing had taken on a menacing quality.

Jesse stood frozen in place, not daring to move an inch. It wasn't a greedy impulse, but fear that commanded his actions now. He looked back at the deer. Its soulless, vacant eyes bore into him as if their nothingness held a tremendous warning he'd failed to heed.

"I will leave you to your prize," Jesse announced, hoping the lurker in the undergrowth would understand his meaning and let him depart without incident.

After waiting for a minute, Jesse began backing towards the trees. His eyes continuously scanned the area, pre-empting the signs of an attack.

Nothing.

The tree line was now within arm's reach; just a few more steps and he would be free of this unseen hunter.

The hairs on Jesse's arm stood erect, preventing him from taking the last lunge backwards. He turned, sensing the danger now lay directly behind him.

The attack came fast.

A blur of orange and black exploded from the undergrowth.

The mound of muscle and fur barrelled into Jesse, knocking him into the clearing.

Long yellow claws ripped at his exposed chest, splashing crimson blood across the grass.

Jesse was instantly aware of the pain overwhelming his nervous system. He quickly comprehended the immense proportion of his foe as its weight crushed him. With its blazing orange coat and deathly yellow eyes, the tiger loomed over him like an ancient jungle god.

It bared its teeth, then roared.

The shock and fear passed quickly. Jesse's survival instincts kicked in.

The tiger's menacing canines gleamed in the sun as it thrust them towards Jesse's throat.

His fingers moved like lightning, catching the beast's head by its upper and lower jaws. Saliva ran across his hands and down his arms as the beast struggled to finish its prey.

It moved, its claws slicing across Jesse's stomach. His skin tore and his muscles convulsed, but he didn't relinquish his grip. Even the merest flinch now could spell his end. Jesse didn't want to be like the deer only a few feet away, a lifeless corpse in the forest, a victim to a superior predator.

"I... am... the... predator!" Jesse screamed, mustering all his strength as he pulled the big cat's jaws apart. He could feel the sinew in its mouth stretch and its bones snap as he pulled.

The tiger relented, rearing in surprise and jumping free of Jesse's dangerous hands. It shook its head vigorously in its agony.

Emboldened, Jesse scrambled to his feet. He looked down

and saw the rips on his stomach healing already, albeit slowly. The tiger's claws had dug deep.

He caught his breath as he surveyed his foe. The tiger had to be triple his weight.

He splayed his arms out in a vain attempt to appear bigger. The tiger roared as if dismissing Jesse's display as pathetic. It was the king of this land and couldn't be frightened so easily.

The tiger eyed him with more than contempt now. There was intrigue in its sparkling eyes. Its protracted claws scraped the earth as it bore its fangs.

This time, Jesse was ready for the leap. He saw the beast's muscle tense before it sprang from the grass. The cat sailed past Jesse as he dived right, losing his footing and landing hard on his shoulder. He felt it dislocate, the pain proving momentarily disorienting.

The tiger spun. Its teeth found Jesse's left calf, puncturing through skin and muscle down to the bone.

Jesse aimed an ungainly kick into the side of the tiger's head with his free leg, freeing his mutilated calf from its maw.

Again on the ground, with a now useless left leg and dangling right arm, Jesse couldn't get back to his feet. Worse still, the tiger was rounding on him again, greedily eyeing his neck. It knew what it had to do to subdue him, whereas Jesse had no idea how to escape the beast.

"Get away!" Jesse gasped as his shoulder popped back into place. He noticed that his leg wasn't healing.

The tiger swatted at Jesse with its powerful forelimbs. Its claws cut through his shattered body like he was made of butter.

Jesse's face was splashed with swathes of his own blood. The red liquid burned in his eyes, temporarily blinding him.

The wind changed.

The tiger's head pushed through Jesse's arms and towards his oesophagus. He knew it was moving to end this fight. Jesse blocked his neck with his forearm, feeling the bone snap as the tiger clamped down on it.

This was life or death. Jesse had no intention of submitting to the beast's will, no matter how much pain it inflicted upon him. His free hand searched for the cat's eye socket, finding it quickly. Jesse pushed his thumb and forefinger into the tiger's eye, feeling something give, like a blood vessel bursting, then a howl of pain. The tiger released its jaw from Jesse's mutilated arm and doubled back.

Jesse was satisfied he'd finally been able to injure this sturdy foe. Hopefully, it would be enough to drive the beast away...

The tiger roared, and Jesse roared back at it. His broken forearm wasn't healing at all. It simply dangled, useless and limp. Jesse couldn't defend himself any longer. If the tiger chose to strike again, it could all be over.

The tiger shook its head violently, then pounced back into the brush. The vegetation trembled, then went still. Jesse breathed a welcome sigh of relief. It seemed that for now at least, the fight was over. He couldn't stay here though, yet he was helpless to move.

There was a clicking sound as the bones in his forearm re-joined. Jesse screamed in agony as this unexpected act brought him near to unconsciousness. Then, rather unexpectedly, Jesse laughed. His supernatural healing factor wasn't completely depleted. Somehow, once again, despite difficult odds, he'd walk out of this.

After twenty minutes, Jesse was able to pull himself to his feet. Then, after an hour of limping, he began to walk again.

Jesse scrambled back up the ridge, away from the tiger's kingdom, with a newfound respect for the other monsters of the forest. He'd begun to think himself above the natural world and it was as if the tiger had appeared to remind him that wasn't the case.

Jesse, a supernatural monster, had almost been killed by a large cat. There was a lesson in there for him to digest, but not before a long period of healing had taken place.

Any delusion that the forest was now his home was shattered. He did not belong anywhere.

CHAPTER EIGHT DRUMS

Jesse was a wreck of a man. His only companions were the chirps of unseen birds and the shuffling shadows of monkeys high in the treetops.

For a time, before the tiger, he'd embraced being one with nature. The diversity of the jungle was endless, and Jesse had become a part of its ecosystem. He could smell, hear and see so clearly now. A clarity that was almost spiritual in nature enveloped him, or so he'd thought. Jesse wasn't like a child suckling at the teat of the Earth, he was an unwelcome parasite in a foreign land.

He knew he didn't truly belong and never could. A deep, irrepressible part of his psyche longed for the comforts and regularity of civilisation. The animals avoided him, smelling his unnatural affliction. This only served to reinforce Jesse's feeling of absolute isolation.

The struggle for survival had become an all-consuming objective. One mistake could spell doom, though Jesse had numerous advantages. His injuries, no matter how grievous, healed quickly. He'd fallen down steep embankments, accidentally impaled himself on a branch and been shot at when he'd stumbled across poachers. Yet, he always recovered as if nothing had happened. Jesse's body was racked with additional scars besides the werewolf wounds. He'd quickly learned that his magic healing factor had a limit, and he had to be careful not to exceed it.

Jesse's hair was long and matted with mud. He had a scraggly beard dominating the lower portion of his face and neck. He could hardly recognise himself when he caught glimpses of his gaunt figure in the still forest pools. Who was this emaciated stranger staring up at him with wild eyes?

His diet mostly consisted of rats. He longed for home-cooked meals and a warm place to rest, but it wasn't meant to be. He was a monster and not fit to be in society any longer.

And yet, thoughts of family and friends couldn't escape him. He wondered where Josh was now. Was he still a lab rat? At least Jesse had his freedom…

Months passed in loneliness and dread for Jesse Billiau. His transformations always left him disoriented and confused, but at least he didn't wake up surrounded by innocent victims. The werewolf inside seemed content to hunt in the forest during the full moon. Its long-range wanderings kept Jesse far from the reach of the AST, who'd almost caught up with him once or twice. Jesse stuck to the deepest, thickest parts of the jungle to avoid being tracked. Whenever he heard vehicles, he took it as an indication that he was going the wrong way. He never stayed in one place too long.

The more that Jesse became lost in the wilderness of Southeast Asia, the more lost he became with himself. He didn't even know if he was in Vietnam anymore. When he'd stumbled near villages, quite by accident, he'd heard different languages and dialects.

It was better that he didn't know where he was. If he didn't know, how could the AST?

Liam Sager's scowling face was burned into Jesse's brain. While he couldn't live in society, he still refused to be a lab rat. Jesse was a monster, cursed to live among the beasts of the land. This was his life.

• • • • •

ON AN UNCOMFORTABLY WARM NIGHT, Jesse was woken by an odd sound.

There was a series of far-off hollers and hoots carrying on the breeze. It was as if a monumental party was happening out in the forest, but that was impossible. Jesse was sure he was far beyond the reach of human habitation.

Jesse got to his feet, listening keenly. It wasn't just sound. There were smells, too; the aroma of people... dozens of people. His tiredness quickly abated as this new mystery revealed itself.

Jesse had adapted to the night. He could see well enough and found a thick tree to climb. As he burst through the pitch-black canopy, he was met by an orange glow igniting the night. It looked like a large bonfire in a distant clearing, only a few kilometres away at most.

This odd occurrence had to be investigated. Jesse considered the possibility of poachers, though that was unlikely. They never willingly invited their own discovery. This party was so obvious and loud it had to be something else.

Jesse pulled a tattered tunic over his head. He'd found it after his last transformation, and it was now his only piece of clothing.

Jesse breathed in, letting odour particles flood his nostrils. He caught the scent and now had to navigate the dark paths of the jungle.

• • • • •

THE JOURNEY WAS QUICK. Jesse stayed clear of the chattering voices from the disparate groups moving in the gloom. There were parties of no more than five people heading towards the bonfire from all directions, guided by torchlight.

The people made a lot of noise, apparently wholly unconcerned with masking their presence out here. Stranger still were the words they uttered, sounding alien to Jesse. There was something about these wanderers in the night that Jesse found unsettling, as if to be in their vicinity was to trespass into an ancient and unknown sin.

Where they converged it was a madness unlike Jesse had ever seen. This meeting in the forest had no organisation or structure other than the enormous circle of fire burning amongst the trees. As soon as the men and women were bathed in the orange warmth from the tall, manicured flames, they undressed and moved into a mass of dancing people.

Jesse couldn't make any sense of this. The people flailed and danced in the firelight as if gripped with unhinged ecstasy. They spasmed and gyrated to a tune without melody or rhythm.

Drums beat and flutes played with no unity or precision. It was just raw, unfiltered noise.

Jesse watched a man stumble past, his eyes rolling in his skull and foam dripping from his mouth.

He noticed that the braver madmen would throw themselves through the wall of fire into an obscured inner circle. Jesse felt the acute pull of the mystery here, part of him wanting to throw away his tunic and join in to investigate. Another voice in his brain warned against such an action. It was like he was in the presence of a horrific power, one that shouldn't be made aware of him.

A hand touched Jesse's shoulder, almost causing him to leap in fright. He swallowed his fear as a shadow slithered into place beside him; a shadow that took on a familiar form.

Jesse recognised the skull mask of Baron Samedi. The God of the Dead was back.

"I need to see what is inside the ring of fire," Jesse began to explain, pausing as he processed the sound of his voice.

"Now, now, Jesse Billiau," Baron Samedi whispered, a hint of warning in his voice, "this is not a place for exploration."

"But surely this is Voodoo? This madness of it? This is your religion!"

The thought had occurred to Jesse when he saw the wildness of the people. It also helped to explain Baron Samedi's presence in Southeast Asia.

"What do you know of Voodoo?" the god asked.

Jesse paused. He actually knew nothing about the Haitian religion. The image of a doll with pins poking through it popped into his head.

"Nothing, really," Jesse mumbled.

Baron Samedi didn't appear to find Jesse's ignorance insulting.

"The first Voodoo temples were built where African slaves ran away to pray. It is also a religion heavily linked with nature. The people invite the deities of the rivers, valleys and mountains into their bodies and make covenants with them. Then they dance in the sacred places. That is not what we are witnessing here."

"I thought you said they worshipped the Christian God?"

"I'm glad you remember," the Baron nodded. "Yes, God is the supreme deity of Voodoo. But the old African gods act as guiding spirits to my followers. In Voodoo, everything that happens is due to the direct intervention of the spirits, whether good or bad. The people make offerings and the spirits take possession for a short time."

"And that isn't this?"

"No. There are no gods here. Just a call to the void and the malevolent things that squirm in the dark."

The way the Baron said it made Jesse shudder. It was good to know that his gut instinct hadn't been wrong about this gathering. This wasn't a wholesome place to be.

"I think it is time I continued telling you my story, as we are not at risk of being overheard here."

Jesse watched the people dancing as he prepared to let his mind absorb the Baron's words.

"I told you of my Brigette, the great flame that changed my destiny. If you remember, I was an agent of Hell, causing chaos. Mamam Brigette served the Church, though I never told you why.

Why would a god of the old world be willing to serve the power that destroyed her home and ended her way of life? Because she saw a greater threat, a secret threat lingering out of view of even the angels. This ritual here is that very same threat.

"It began in colonial Africa. Brother sold brother into slavery. Humans were traded as mere possessions across the world, deemed of lesser value because of unchangeable physical attributes. Despair ran rampant as atrocities became normal life. In that despair and in that hopelessness, something dark festered. Long tentacles found anchor in the weakened minds of the oppressed and tortured, and manipulated them through dreams. Mamam Brigette showed me the dances in the firelight. She let me hear the beating drums and piping flutes in the dark. The calls to dark deities filled my ears and I dismissed them. She warned me of powers beyond God himself, and I laughed at the notion. Then, I met him..."

Jesse couldn't help but notice that Baron Samedi looked incredibly grim.

"Who?"

"The Sundered King, he called himself. A lonely figure who walked in the remote places of the world. He sought out the disenfranchised and the lost. Wherever he appeared, these rituals began."

"What was he? A god like you?" Jesse asked.

"To this day, I can't be sure. He was a broken figure, in service to something greater than himself, something that viewed all life as a game... It was in Haiti that we met, during a period of great unrest. Mamam Brigette warned me not to engage with such a fellow. His hatred of the gods was palpable. But, I was a Knight of Hell, so what did I care? A fallen angel of mighty God... What he showed me was terrifying beyond God or Satan, beyond anything in this small world.

"I knew that I couldn't let the people fall under his spell. The beliefs of the Church had been pushed on the people of Haiti, though unsuccessfully. I turned my efforts to aiding Mamam Brigette to draw the masses away from the Sundered King's infestation and to God, the lesser of two evils. It didn't work. The fires grew as the people continued to dance, inviting things from the void into their minds. That's when I changed tact. I asked Mamam Brigette to help me recruit the gods of Africa, those who'd survived, to blend the old and the new. I let the people continue to dance, but instead, they would invite the gods of their ancestors into their bodies. Heaven pardoned the African gods and allowed this new religion to form, as prayer was still going to the one God. Voodoo was born in earnest, and it was for this that I earned my apotheosis. The people came to see me as their god of life and death, and I became it, shedding the name Samyaza and becoming Samedi."

"But, this evil religion of the Sundered King is happening right here, right now," Jesse began, feeling somewhat like he was missing the point. "You only stopped it in a small part of the world, but not everywhere."

"This sickness has infested all of human history. In time, you will help us stop it, but that time is not now."

Jesse watched the mad flailing of the dancers in silence for a long moment. Clearly, the machinations of the gods wasn't something he was meant to understand easily.

"So... this isn't Voodoo," Jesse concluded lamely, after processing the god's words.

"This is older than Voodoo. This dance is unhinged and chaotic, born of dark dreams from sunken places. It serves no purpose, other than allowing the body to release itself to the true primal."

Jesse couldn't help but notice the angst with which Baron Samedi spoke. It was almost as if he feared these people.

"Who are they? Where have they come from?" Jesse asked. He couldn't help but be intimidated by the fire reflectively dancing on the Baron's death mask.

"Everywhere and nowhere..."

"Are you being deliberately vague?" Jesse sighed, annoyed.

"Yes," Baron Samedi smiled. "Your mind is fragile, and you are touched by forces beyond the natural order. This is a bad place for you to be right now. The fact that the cult is active here means that your time in the jungle must end."

"Are you going to help me?" Jesse asked. He was immensely confused as to why this self-proclaimed god had appeared three times, only for Jesse's life to get worse after each visit.

"I will help as any friend would, with some advice," the Baron responded.

"What advice?"

"The forest is dangerous. After the next full moon, it would be in your best interest to return to society."

"You know what I've done... my hands are soaked in the blood of the innocent! This is where I belong, away from society..."

"Things are changing. The festival we look upon is proof of that. Take the advice of the God of the Dead."

The pair paused as a chant emerged among the dancers. It grew louder and louder as more of the wild people joined the chorus. The words again were utterly alien to Jesse, though he did pick up on some of the phrases being repeated. There was Yog-Sothoth, Nyarlathotep and Cthulhu... phrases that meant nothing to him. However, they seemed to release a new wave of ecstasy through the convulsing dancers.

"Be warned, Jesse, that a time will come when you will seek me out. Go to Haiti. Find the black goats. They will lead you to me."

"I don't understand," Jesse began but was cut off by the Baron.

"I think it would be unwise for you to mention our meetings here. The river of time does not always flow in its proper direction and I'd rather its disruptions not drown us all."

While Jesse didn't understand the Baron's meaning, he could tell the seriousness of his words.

Jesse noticed a man in a hooded robe moving through the crowd. Cradled in his arms was a small statue carved from a strange green material. The hooded man walked swiftly out of sight, moving through the ring of flame before Jesse could garner what the idol represented.

"Flee from this place, Jesse Billiau, lest unnumbered eyes fall upon you," the God of the Dead warned.

Then, Baron Samedi was gone.

Jesse decided to heed the god's words. He silently crept away from the fire and the noise of the drums.

Was the Baron right? Should he at last approach civilisation again? How he longed to be free of the mud and the rain. To eat properly cooked food...

He would find somewhere safe to sleep, then consider it in the morning. There wasn't much time, as his next transformation was approaching with the growing face of the moon.

CHAPTER NINE RUSSIAN

- 2020 -
RURAL CAMBODIA

O n what he assumed to be another unremarkable morning, Jesse was strolling through a pocket of broad-leaf ferns when an unfamiliar smell filtered into his nostrils. There was chicken, rice and abundant spices... it was the smell of properly cooked food, meaning people were nearby.

"I can't go," Jesse shook his head. It'd been so long since he'd interacted with another person that he was afraid he wouldn't know how anymore. Was he even a man, or was he a thing of the forest?

Yet, he couldn't help the voice of Baron Samedi ringing in his ears. The time to return was coming... though that encounter had been weeks ago now.

Despite his best intentions to remain a ghost in the forest, Jesse had slowly begun edging back towards his humanity. He'd taken shelter in abandoned ruins instead of beneath the endless trees. And not just because the ruins provided food, mainly in the form of abundant vermin scurrying about, but due to something deeper in his subconscious. The pull for the sounds, sights and tastes of civilisation grew stronger in him by the day.

Jesse paused and contemplated the foreign smell he'd come across. It was a fragrant curry. Something delightful was being prepared and it was a powerful enticer. He could almost see himself as an old-school cartoon character, letting the wafting odour pick him up and carry him to its source.

A slave to his base desire to eat a meal that wasn't raw rodent, Jesse wrapped his tattered cloak around himself and pulled the hood up, masking his face in shadow. His heightened senses told him in which direction to travel.

He emerged from the forest at the edge of a rice plantation. The stalks were small and vibrantly green, with many drowned in the puddles that dominated the field.

Some distance away, a man was pushing a strange device along the rows of crops. It was a tractor motor on wooden wheels with two long handles. Jesse watched him curiously, and not just for the man's actions. It'd been so long since he'd seen another person it was like looking at the illusion of a thing he'd forced himself to erase all memory of.

Islands of trees emerged periodically throughout the rice field, and Jesse decided to use them to mask his approach. Different areas of the field had been fenced off, though 'fence' was hardly the right word. Sticks and branches, collected from the forest without any regard for their uniformity of shape and size, had been stuck in the mud and linked with loops of rope and fishing wire. These were no impediments to Jesse.

A series of wooden buildings, like incomplete open-faced sheds, sat at the edge of the field. If he could reach them, he would surely come across a road.

Hunger had awoken in Jesse like a sleeping beast roaring to life. God was he ever hungry. His mind made up, he began his dart through the mud and water to the closest island of trees.

Jesse made it to the sheds undetected, except by the chickens, who clucked in annoyance at his proximity to their coop. Several stray dogs growled but wouldn't come near him, which Jesse was thankful for. Fighting animals had proven to be a most unpleasant experience.

A dirt road connected the shed with a thin patch of distant forest. The smell of food was stronger here. He quickly determined that he had to follow the road back into the sparse jungle to find its source. Jesse could see the optimistic blue sky stretching for miles around, unimpeded by tall trees.

The new and rather hopeless optimism in him had him believing that heading towards the town was the right choice, and Jesse didn't protest this inner voice.

It took half an hour of cautious walking before Jesse arrived at the settlement. Hiding in the forest was removed as an option, as there weren't enough trees to conceal his haggard form. Jesse had to reveal his dirty, shaggy, tattered figure to the world. As he ducked past shrines erected on poles and slinked by the cows that wandered the streets, Jesse couldn't help but feel a slight embarrassment at how he must look.

The rustic village was serene in its simplicity, and so very green. Of the half dozen or so people he encountered, none paid him any heed, other than an odd look here or there.

As the road widened, leading back out into the wilderness,

Jesse found the source of the tempting odour. A two-story building, looking suspiciously like a pub, rose from the jungle as an inviting giant welcoming him.

Jesse had to forget his greed and hunger for a moment. There were more smells, though not the stink of the jungle with which he was so acquainted. Something was out of place...

Jesse walked the circumference of the building and quickly found the oddity. Two vehicles, polished, though splashed with mud, were sitting by the main entry. They did not fit the usual transports he'd seen out here as they were modern and expensive. Through the rear windows, he could see that they were jam-packed with boxes and boxes of equipment. Several crates were marked with a familiar logo, one he'd seen before.

"iHeal Genetics," Jesse murmured, his eyes widening in wonderment.

Perhaps the man... what was his name? Napier! That was it, and the woman, Mia, were back. The slaughter at the drug-runner's compound could've ruined their plans entirely. If they were here now, did that mean there were other options for them in Southeast Asia?

Desire to know and to untangle this mysterious thread burned in him.

Still, Jesse submitted to caution as he surveyed the building's access and egress points.

He avoided the main entry and found a side door. It was locked, though a little effort saw the wooden latch splinter easily. He crept down a dark hall and into the main entertaining area. It was a bar. Liquors, dull with dust, were stacked on hand-crafted shelves behind a long bench top. Several men, looking to be farmers, sat near the bar in huddled conversation.

Not far from them, at a round table, sat three foreigners. Jesse didn't recognise any of them, though noted that they were equally absorbed in their own discussion.

Light filtered in through the windows, illuminating only certain portions of the expanse. There were many dark corners to hide in here, even for a silhouette as large as his. Jesse wondered if the villagers ever sat in the shadows and discussed conspiracies, as this seemed the perfect venue to do so. Today, the secretive voids of light would serve him in his mission of discovery.

Jesse slunk along the wall towards the foreigners and sat down. He was well within eavesdropping distance, though much to his disappointment, the conversation was in Russian.

Suddenly feeling foolish and very exposed, Jesse got up, intending to leave, when he was noticed.

"You there!" a jarring Russian voice called.

Jesse froze, his stomach doing summersaults. He didn't need to turn to know that he was the focus of the remark.

"You are a foreigner in these lands, too?"

Jesse nodded reluctantly, ensuring his hood still covered his face.

"Come and sit with us. Do not take this as an insult, but you appear well acquainted with these lands."

Jesse paused, considering his options. His inner voice screamed at him to run, but he couldn't trust that voice anymore. For too long it'd been removed from the world of people.

Then, the food arrived.

Jesse salivated as the exotic aromas danced through his nostrils.

He must've looked like a starved puppy, as the Russian who'd called on him seized on this opportunity with unexpected fervour.

"You look hungry. I will order another plate. You take mine."

Jesse's body betrayed his mind as he moved to the table, a slave to desire. He sat down, and without a word, put his face to the bowl. Like a beast gorging itself from a trough, he ate with no dignity. Jesse consumed the meal like what he'd become, a thing of the woods.

When he raised his face from the bowl, feeling satisfied like he hadn't in months, he finally took in the men's appearances.

Only the centre person, who'd called him, had a cheery demeanour. He was bespectacled and scrawny, whereas the other two looked serious and battle-hardened. It wasn't a stretch of logic to assume that they could've been the skinny man's bodyguards. The serious pair assessed Jesse with a reproachful gaze as if they'd just witnessed an illicit display without being allowed to consent.

The cheery man, however, raised a hand when Jesse was done.

"Viktor Petrov," he smiled.

Jesse grunted in response. He didn't want to give his name.

"And you are?"

"Steve," Jesse mumbled after a noticeable pause, not sounding remotely convincing.

"Well, Steve, I must say, we did not expect to see any other foreigners out here. You must have quite the story to tell," Viktor chatted animatedly. He looked young, around Jesse's age, if not a little older.

Jesse observed his own yellowed nailbeds, painfully conscious of how dirty he was. If the Russian had noticed Jesse's wretched appearance, he didn't comment on it, almost as if he expected this.

"Where are we," Jesse asked quietly, his voice hoarse and raspy from lack of use.

Viktor didn't react to the oddity of the question. "Cambodia," he answered casually. "Very rural Cambodia."

"Cambodia," Jesse repeated. "Why are you here?"

"We are looking for some old ruins. Here, I will show a picture."

Viktor handed Jesse his phone, which displayed an image of a crumbling temple. Jesse had come across it days ago. He considered it an obvious landmark and had stayed well clear ever since.

Viktor was able to read Jesse's face. "You have seen it," he grinned.

"Yes," Jesse nodded, not bothering to lie. "Why do you want to go there?"

Viktor seemed flummoxed by the question as if the answer was so obvious Jesse was a fool to ask. It wasn't obvious to Jesse though; why would iHeal Genetics be looking for an old temple?

"I am a scientist who studies these kinds of things," Viktor shrugged, almost trying too hard to seem unconcerned.

Jesse eyed him warily. Viktor noticed, and desiring to appear completely non-threatening, changed tact.

112

"Do you live around here?" he asked politely.

Jesse shrugged and muttered, "My business, not yours."

Viktor smiled. The boy was cocky, and Jesse didn't like that. He had an air of academic success about him that made him false and untrustworthy.

Jesse abruptly stood up. "I need to go. Thank you for the food."

Viktor rose to his feet, motioning to the two other men to stay down. The bodyguards now appeared on the edge of their seats, waiting to spring into action on Viktor's command.

"Wait. We could use a man of your knowledge. Take us to the temple and I can pay you handsomely for your efforts."

Jesse shook his head.

"I can offer you more than money. What do you want?" Viktor asked plainly, his quivering voice betraying a hint of desperation.

"To be left alone," Jesse stated, intending that to end the discussion.

"Then I can help you!" Viktor exclaimed, his eyes lighting up. "I do not wish to cast unjust aspersions upon you, but we know that a fugitive is being hunted by the Australian Government through these lands. It does not take a detective to work out it is you."

"Prove it," Jesse hissed, taking a step from the table.

"I mean," Viktor continued quickly, "that we do not care what crimes you have committed. If you help us, we can help you. The Australians are like dogs to your scent, as I'm sure you're aware. The forest cannot hide you forever."

Jesse paused. It was, of course, common knowledge that he

was being hunted. The Australians had given out pamphlets with his face on them. Perhaps the Russians were his final escape from the AST. Perhaps this is why Baron Samedi had directed him towards civilisation.

Still, something about this didn't feel right in his gut...

"Okay," Jesse announced, ending the biting silence at the table. "What would you have me do?"

"We will meet you at the edge of the road leading out of the village, once we collect and prepare our equipment, though it will take some time. If you'd like, we can offer you lodgings here?"

"No," Jesse snapped. He would retreat back into the forest through the night. It wasn't safe here. He was known here.

"Ah, right, well... tomorrow morning, then. Meet at first light."

Jesse nodded his agreement and began moving for the door. Again, Viktor's bodyguards looked to be restraining themselves from getting up and pursuing Jesse.

With as much haste as he could muster, Jesse fled the town. The more he considered this idea, the more he liked it. He could get up before dawn's first light and scout the meeting point. If anything was amiss, he simply wouldn't show.

Perhaps the Russians could get him out of Southeast Asia altogether. Drop him off somewhere he could start a new life... Though it'd have to be somewhere he was no danger to the innocent.

He'd figure it out tomorrow. For now, Jesse would go back into the trees and enjoy the feeling of fullness in his belly.

• • • • •

WHETHER IT WAS THE FOOD or the thought of an escape from the forest, Jesse wasn't sure, but something caused him to oversleep. The morning calls of the forest birds woke him as light breached the dense wall of vegetation.

Jesse scrambled out of the ferns and threw on his stinking clothes. He had to get to the rendezvous point fast or risk the Russians leaving without him.

He crossed the rice field with zeal and moved towards the village at a running jog. Stealth was no longer his concern.

The sun hung low over the trees when he arrived at the village. Jesse barely noticed the abundant tyre tracks digging into the dirt road, nor paid attention to the absence of the villagers. He was singularly focused on not being left behind. The looming shadow of the AST was always behind him, and at last, he could be free of it for good.

Jesse came to the point of the road where it widened and swung his head left to right.

There was no one here! He'd missed them...

Then, a voice with a strong Russian accent sprang up from a nearby house. "You are late," Viktor called, sounding nervous.

Jesse began to murmur his apologies but paused as an array of odours filled his nostrils. He smelled weapons... and something he'd experienced of the AST... silver...

Men were emerging from the buildings all around. Rifles were raised and pointed right at him. These were not drug-runners, but soldiers, or mercenaries. It was painfully apparent by their uniforms that they weren't AST either.

The circle of men closed in on Jesse, who raised his fists defiantly.

"Do not fight," a new female voice called, as a woman stepped out from behind one of the armed men.

Jesse recognised her instantly. This was Mia, the iHeal Genetics representative he'd seen in the compound all those months ago.

"What is this?" Jesse asked through gritted teeth.

"An end to your reign of terror in these lands," Mia answered excitedly, her eyes alight with anticipation. "When Viktor said he'd let you go yesterday, I was almost ready to eject him from the program. Thank god you returned this morning."

"You're handing me to the AST?" Jesse grimaced.

"Oh no. You will be coming with us; in what manner will be up to you."

"Why?" Jesse asked, the panic rising in his voice. Mia spoke with the clarity of someone who knew exactly who she was talking to.

"There was an information leak. We know what the Australian Government captured. And we know of the Australians' activities in these lands. When we put two-and-two together, we determined what they were hunting. You are a werewolf, are you not?"

Jesse didn't react. He'd been so foolish. He'd been senseless. His long isolation had warped his judgement, and now he'd pay for it.

"What are you going to do with me?"

"Science that is almost magic," Mia sighed as if she was in love with the concept.

Viktor now jutted in, "I recognised you immediately yesterday, of course. Very fortuitous that you should appear right where we are, but we were not ready. I know you are dangerous, and did not want to risk you killing us and escaping."

Jesse snorted with derision. He scanned the area round and round, but couldn't see anything... no way to escape...

"Will you come quietly?" Mia asked.

The circle of soldiers was getting tighter. The stench of their sweat and the reek of their silver accoutrements consumed Jesse.

"No," Jesse stated, lunging at the nearest man with his fists clenched.

His target rolled backwards and fired two rounds into Jesse's shoulder. Jesse gasped with pain and gripped the sizzling wound. The bullets weren't silver, and as soon as they entered his skin, Jesse could feel his super-human body working to spit them back out.

There was a flurry of activity as weapons were released to their slings and shining silver batons were drawn by a handful of the mercenaries.

They began whacking Jesse's arms and legs with ferocity. Jesse fought back as best as he could, but the blunt instruments carried a debilitating bite as if they were coated in poison. Each strike further infected him. Jesse's left femur broke beneath a barrage of powerful blows and seemed resistant to immediate healing. His left forearm snapped as he braced against another swing.

Jesse collapsed in a crumpled heap in the middle of the road.

Here, in rural Cambodia, he was defeated.

An order to cease was given, and the blurry face of Mia appeared in Jesse's fading vision.

"Big things are happening. You will be the cornerstone of the scientific revolution coming. Oh, and don't worry, we will have the other Australian werewolf in good time, too. He will be the final product if our tests on you fail."

There was no maliciousness in Mia's voice, just a chilling sense of purpose.

An unnerving calm came over Jesse. He saw the image of Baron Samedi's skull mask flash across his vision as if the god was commanding him not to fight anymore. Gods or no gods, it didn't matter. Jesse knew that his time for revenge would come, and he'd seize the moment when it did.

THE STORY CONTINUES IN:

THE OLD WORLD SAGA BOOK THREE:

IN THE SHADOW

OF THE

OLD WORLD

THE OLD WORLD SAGA SO FAR...

BOOK ONE: IN THE SHADOW OF MONSTROUS THINGS

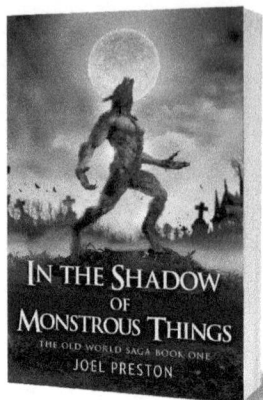

A European holiday takes a sinister turn when Joshua Dare encounters a werewolf. Feeling its bite, Josh escapes, but soon realises that he is now inflicted with an ancient curse. Having to learn how to manage his full moon affliction, Josh is thrust into a world of secret organisations, government operatives and mysterious strangers hunting him. Josh has entered a larger story of gods and monsters, and this is just the beginning...

BOOK TWO: RISE GOLDEN APOLLO

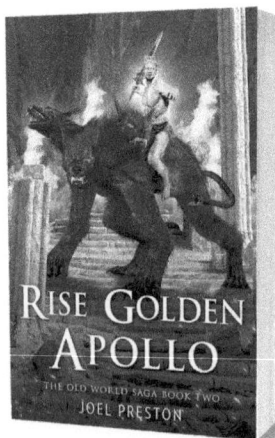

An Australian spy, Melissa Pythia, is searching for a powerful artefact in Rome. More than underworld figures are on her trail as she learns about her connection to a golden sword.

At the same time, in the distant past, the gods of the Underworld are waging war against the angels of Heaven. The surprise attack on the Olympians leaves Apollo lost in time, and only Melissa can bring him back...

Novella Two: THE WENDIGO INCIDENT

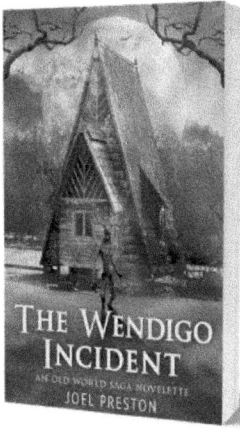

Something has angered a supernatural terror in the forests of Minnesota, and the US Government needs help dealing with it. Fortunately, rumours have reached them that the Australians have captured a werewolf. Sometimes to kill a monster, you need a monster of your own. Now, Joshua Dare is off to the USA to assist in bringing down one of Native American folklore's greatest monsters - the wendigo. Other sinister things seem to be happening in that forest too....

Book Three: IN THE SHADOW OF THE OLD WORLD

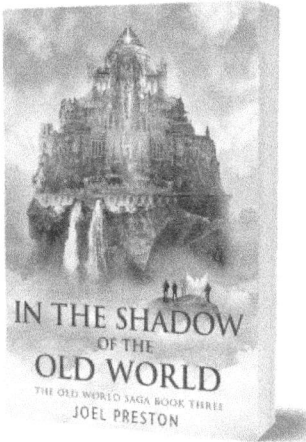

Fearing an information leak and seeking to bolster their alliance with The Old World, the Australian Government has moved Josh Dare to Japan. He is soon tracked down by malevolent supernatural forces who want to exploit his curse. He is the best link to the empty position of Zeus, the vanished god-king. Now, a small team of Australian and US operatives need to work with the gods of old to fulfill an ancient ritual and stop that power falling into the wrong hands.

Novella Three: EARTH'S MIGHTIEST WARRIOR

Long ago lived a warrior renowned as the greatest to ever live. Sigurd of the Volsung line has had his story told through the ages, though not all of it. It was thought his tale ended with his death, but then came the war of gods and angels. Now, Sigurd survives as a rat and a champion in Lucifer's new Hell. The tale of Earth's mightiest warrior is only half told. The new legend of Sigurd takes him across the fiery planes of the Underworld, with beings far beyond Norse myth, on his greatest adventure yet.

Book Four: FALL SILVER ARTEMIS

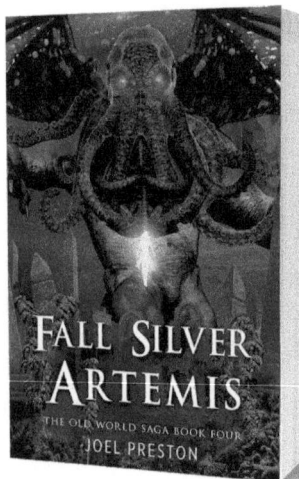

Danni Quinn has completed her training and is on her first mission. The goal: finding an artefact of the lost God Zeus. Danni and her boss, the reincarnated Oracle of Delphi, Melissa Pythia, set out to find the Goddess Artemis. Travelling across the scorched plains of Hell they meet the long dead hero, Sigurd the Volsung, who agrees to aide them on their quest. Danni's team heads down a path towards sunken cities and alien horrors. With the help of her former flame, Joshua Dare, and the rest of the AST, Danni will risk everything to complete her mission…

Randall Dare thought he was solving a complex equation. Little did he know that the act of writing some numbers on blackboard would catapult him across dimensions to a strange realm known as the Dark World.

Now, as he works to find a way home, he must face off against the monstrous octopus-headed aliens, cosmic gods and the mysterious creatures that call the bizarre planet home. And time is ticking, as Randall is carrying a warning that needs to reach the team back on Earth. Something dreadful has woken up, and his new allies can help to stop it...

WITH MORE COMING SOON!

Milton Keynes UK
Ingram Content Group UK Ltd.
UKHW012223290324
440241UK00001B/70

9 780645 779134